MW01127975

Tina- A basketball wife at the end of her rope. She decides that she is done dealing with her husband's infidelities. She files for divorce and finds love in her lawyer's arms. When her estranged husband gives her an ultimatum, will she go back to what she knows or follow her heart to freedom.

Bobbi- An artist and college professor has a secret. She is married to the abusive son of a senator. When he does the unthinkable, she had had enough and leaves. But will he allow her to live without him?

.

Kenna-A successful lawyer who yearns for love. She has one important rule. *"Do not date co-workers.* Will she forget her rule when love is standing in front of her? Or let love pass her by.

****

This is book one of four. The "If He Loved You" series. There are three subsequent books that follow. Each focusing on each individual friend and their lives following this story. Stay Tuned and ENJOY!!!

****

Tina

I stood next to the bed staring at his stupid face. I wasn't sure if I wanted to laugh or rip his face off. I had just received another email from one of his mistresses. You would think that as a millionaire ball player he would want to, at some point, start learning to cover his tracks.

I guess, to be honest, I could take some of the blame. *Why?* Well, because you teach people how to treat you. Apparently, my lesson to this man was that I would accept his cheating ways. So, why shouldn't he sleep around with random women? I mean, besides the obvious reason. That reason being that he is married. However, in my attempts to keep our marriage together I had set the bar pretty damn low on this subject. I had always forgiven him and taken him back after his affairs. Not this time. I was seriously over his infidelity.

I personally know of seven of his affairs. He and I had been together since college. I was the one that was down with him when it was Ramen noodles and $0.99 sodas to get through the week. He was the first and only man that I've ever known. It certainly wasn't the same for him.

He wasn't like this in college. Not at first. But then again, he was broke. It was not until it became clear that he would most likely be drafted, that the females started to appear. And even then, I never heard anything about him cheating. Because of this, I trusted him completely.

When we were first married, things were the same. I would actually see women flirting with him. Now though, he looked flattered and even returned some of it. After about three or four years of marriage, I may have started to have my doubts, but never a word was whispered in my presence by these wannabe baller wives. Things were definitely different now. I guess after ten years of marriage he's not even trying to hide it anymore. He thinks the big houses and fancy cars will make me stay. But I'm fed up.

You would think he would want to be more careful. I mean my best friend is an attorney, after all. Also, he has met my mother. He knows she teaches all seven of her girls to get an education and have a plan B. I always listened to my mommy. So, while he was out sleeping around with these little loose booty betties, I was squirreling money away.

If he gave me twenty thousand for a shopping spree, I spent seven and put the rest away into savings and investments. I still, for the life of me, cannot figure out why someone needs to spend that much in one shopping trip. I have always wondered how these wives of ballplayers and millionaires ended up with no money once he left them. I imagine that they are too worried about the wrong things. Don't get it twisted now. I love Vera Wang and Manolo Blahnik as much as the next girl. Though not enough to be stuck in an unhappy marriage for appearance's sake.

I had seen my share of these ladies have to move back home with their parents. I mean, *Que?* Most of the time there was some pre-nuptial agreement which screwed her over. If they had signed one, it was all the more reason to save for a rainy day. To me, this was definitely a Tsunami.

With that being said, I had at least three accounts that he knew nothing about. I also just so happen to own property in my mother's name and the names of some of my sisters. I had rental income coming in that he knew nothing about. Both commercial and residential. I owned a few business parks with convenience stores, restaurants and even doctor's offices. At this point, I was a millionaire by myself.

I was naive about men, money and life when we met. I will give him that. However, he had not married the sweet little fool of a wife that he thought he had. He'd learn soon enough. I was thirty- one and we hadn't had any children yet. I told him that was because I wasn't ready.

He was always on the road and I didn't want to be raising our children alone. It wasn't fair to them, I explained when he would bring it up. The truth was, after the third affair, I had made up my mind that I absolutely, without a shadow of a doubt, did not want to bring a child into this mess.

We had a pregnancy scare after the third affair and I was so damn afraid that I was. I should have been praying that the test came back positive like all the other wives in the association. Yet, all I could think about was, *"what if I had to leave him?"* When the test came back negative, I did a little dance in the bathroom before I came out and showed it to him.

He looked disappointed, which did start to make me feel guilty. Then I thought about if he was feeling guilty about any of his side chicks. Since he would turn around and do it again, I'll take, *"He does not give a damn"*, for two hundred Alex. Once that was more than apparent, I decided that there was no other option for me other than to leave.

I called Kenna, my best friend, and told her I was ready. After she stopped shouting *"Woohooo"*, she told me that she had just the person. Later that week, she had introduced me to a divorce lawyer, Lawrence. We had a meeting coming up on Monday. I printed out every single one of these emails that, I believe her name was Roxy, had sent me.

Not just her emails. Oh no, I printed out the emails, pictures and text from all of the other women as well. I stopped and read some of them.

..so sexy, what you getting into tonight?

Hopefully you.

Won't ur pretty little wife that u were with on the red carpet wit be expecting u...

She don't sweat me like that. She think I'm hanging with my teammates. She trusts me

If only she knew...lol

We don't talk about my wife, remember. Now, Will the door be open?

Amongst other things...lol

Good girl. You know what I like. I will be there in thirty minutes..

I mean, *barf.* He could have at least gotten a burner phone like the drug dealers and mob guys do. But no, he used his phone. The one that he shared a plan with me on. This was why women never got caught and men always did.

If I was having affairs, I would have a van in a storage unit with a bike inside. And at least five different wigs. I would even buy those fake tattoos and piercings. I would drive over to a different city. Then park in like a Target or Wal-Mart parking lot, about three blocks away and then bike to the hotel. That way if said *thundercat* ever saw us out together or on a magazine, he wouldn't even know it was me. But all of that sounds exhausting. Which is why I DO NOT CHEAT!

Whatever they didn't send me as proof, I was able to print offline from the cell phone company. I then put them in my safe. I couldn't have him finding the evidence I was going to use to get my spousal support and half. I always pretended not to believe the mistresses. In an effort to prove themselves, they always sent me his text messages, phone logs, pics and emails. These chicks were going to ruin him.

He didn't even have the good sense to find a girl that was as loyal as I was. It was like they slept with him just so that they could call me. At this point, they could all have him. I can't believe he didn't see it in my eyes every day when I looked at him. The fact that I was utterly done with his lying, conniving, disrespectful, cheating ass went right over his head. I had stopped pretending a long time ago too. I guess if he had really paid me any attention in the last three years he would have noticed. Oh well, he was gonna learn today.

Today, because he was leaving for training camp. He was already packed. Heck, I had packed him as I always did since he was drafted to the National Basketball Association. He did not know that I had already decorated my new condo. The only thing I had left to do was call the movers to come and help me pick up my clothing out of my huge closet. Everything else could stay.

I was not attached to this million-dollar home or the hundreds of thousands of dollars worth of furniture in it. He could have it all. Let Roxy come lay up on the bed or couch. I'm not sure that she hadn't already. I needed a clean break. And I was determined to have it. I wished him the best, but I was over it.

Kenna

I had just tried another case in front of Judge Johnson. I could not stand her. She was not too fond of me either. At least not since she had found out that we were both dating the same circuit court judge a little ways back. Of course, I did not know anything about it at the time. Apparently, she was spending the night at his house and found my electronic planner in his bedroom.

It was left on the nightstand totally by accident. I had received a call as I was packing up to leave. It was my secretary, Miracle. She had added an appointment and wanted to be sure that I had gotten it. When she called, I had just finished putting on my make-up in the bathroom. I rushed out, put my bag on the bed, pulled my planner out and checked it.

That was just around the time he came over to where I was, looking for a morning quickie. I won't lie. He almost found it, but I glanced at the clock and realized I was going to be late for court. I am not one of those women who plants things to be found. That is too childish for my taste.

I think by the time she went into his bathroom and saw my make-up pouch with my name embroidered on the front, that may have been the impression she got. It was not hard to figure out who I was. Not too many *Kennas* with *Mac* and *Fenty* in their makeup bags with planners that say *"court."*

So, there was that. I had been honest and up front about it when she asked me. I then told him I didn't want to see him anymore. It was never that serious for me in any case. He was someone to hang out with when I was bored. But of course, as some women do, she blamed me anyway. Even though they continue to date to this day. I'm also pretty sure she took my *"Trophy wife"* highlighter out of my bag and it hasn't been back in stock online or in stores to this day. I think that made me even more mad than him being a liar and causing me all of this grief.

Ever since all of this has happened, every time I have a case in front of her, she makes my life hell. Not enough that I could prove she was being biased. Because I still did win the cases. I was a beast in the courtroom. No one could deny me that. I presented arguments that could never be disputed. Prosecutors hated to see me coming. I would show up in my heels and expensive suits and I would wear them out.

I always loved to argue. And I hated to see people treated unfairly. That is why I went into law. I absolutely love my job. I wasn't the only African-American female at my practice but I was the only African-American female partner. I had lawyers that could try the cases for me but, I loved the rush of the courtroom.

I had given up a lot for my career. My mother never stopped reminding me of that. I tried to explain to her that lots of women were putting off marriage and babies until their career was at a certain point. But she was old school. She wanted us to be both educated and self- sufficient. But that was only in case our husbands messed up and we needed to take care of ourselves and our children. Plan A was to get a good man, get married and have some babies.

My father was from the old school as well. When *"men were men"* he called it. Even though he was proud that his daughter was a lawyer, he also wanted to see me happily married and settled down with children. To be honest, I wanted that too. There were just a lot of men who couldn't handle the fact that I was so driven. I had flat out had men tell me that.

"Oh, you work too much." Well, they often times worked just as much. Or they had an expectation that if they ever married me, I would transform into a housewife. Uh, that would be a

negative. I did not see why I had to choose if they didn't have to. So here I was, career lit. My love life, not so much.

I had changed my life plan over and over. I was always pushing back the age that I wanted to be married and have children by. Now it was thirty- five. That gave me four years to find Mr. right. Mr. Right would support me in having it all. Once I met him, the rest of the time would be to get to know him, get proposed to, have my dream wedding, and start popping out babies. All while being a partner in the firm. Four years was a lifetime. Or so I kept telling myself to stay positive and motivated. If I didn't do that, I might give up on love all together.

I also had friends who were not in the best marriages. They did not give me a lot of hope on that front. I mean, just because I was a lawyer, it did not mean that I did not want what every girl wanted. I wanted my prince charming riding in on his horse and sweeping me up off my feet. So far all of my friends had married losers, cheaters and abusers. Makes you think there aren't any good men out there. But I was still optimistic, most days.

I headed back to my office. I had to get to work on some briefs and read through some contracts. All of this with deadlines to meet. My client will be glad to hear that we had a settlement coming in as soon as next month.

The company I was up against couldn't deny the facts. They had allowed their employees to be bullied. By law, you cannot allow harassment in the workplace. And now my client would have three million dollars to prove it.

Just as I stepped on the elevator, I received a text message. It was from Jeff. He was congratulating me on another case I had won this week. He was a lawyer at a rival firm. We both attended the same school for law, although he graduated a couple of years after me.

I could not tell a lie, he was sexy. But we have worked together before. I had a rule, never to date coworkers or anyone I had worked with. It limited the pool a little bit. I will admit that. I had my reasons though. The last time I did that, it had cost me my make-up. I wasn't willing to pay that price again.

I won't lie though. Jeff was tempting. Like serpent in the garden tempting. He had a girl thinking like, "*I didn't even think I liked apple's...but a chick is starving.*" Then again, there was the rule.

My best friends, Tina and Bobbi, thought I was absolutely crazy for this rule. They thought there were far too many good-looking and successful black male lawyers for me to limit myself. They were probably right. Though I might add their pickers were a little off.

I had just recently introduced Tina to a colleague of mine who is going to handle her divorce. I can't tell you how glad I was that she was getting away from that lying, cheating and disrespectful loser. I had told her since college not to do it. But she was hardheaded and had to learn the hard way. But I was going to be as supportive as I could. She had always been there for me. She was actually the glue that kept us all together. Now, I was going to do what I could to help her.

Bobbi and her husband were a whole other issue. I couldn't even think about it right now. I would get too upset when it crossed my mind. Any damn part of it. And I had work to do. I headed up to my office and my secretary, Miracle, was waiting for me there.

"Hey Kenna, another win?"

"Of course, you know how we do it."

"And how is judge Johnson?" she inquired.

"Bitter and vindictive as ever. But as usual, her face was beat to perfection and her hair was laid."

"I don't see how you can compliment her with the way she treats you." she added.

"Hey, I'm no hater, you know I love a good face of makeup."

"That you do." She conceded.

"And you also know I was looking for any trace of my highlighter girl."

She laughed before asking, "you still on that?"

"Am I still on that??? Of course, I am. They are still out online and in stores. I'll be on that until something gives."

We both laughed again at my obsession with this highlighter.

"Girl, you are crazy." She reminded me. As if I didn't know.

"I have heard that before. Any messages?"

"They're all on your desk. One is from County General. They called about two minutes before you walked in."

"The hospital? that's odd. Okay. Thank you, hon." I said as I turned to walk into my office.

As I sat my briefcase down, my cell phone rang. It was Tina.

"Hey boo. I was just thinking..." I never managed to finish my sentence.

"Meet me at County, it's Bobbi."

"I'm leaving now."

Bobbi

I lie in that hospital bed for the hundredth time it seemed. Though this was worse, by far, than all of the rest. My obstetrician was using an ultrasound machine trying to find the baby's heartbeat. They had been trying for too long, I thought to myself. When I went in to see the doctors for my regular prenatal check-ups, it never took this long to hear her fast, little heartbeat, singing to me.

Because of that, I already knew what they were about to say. That I had lost the baby. I was trying to brace myself to hear those actual words. I was trying to be strong but failing miserably. I felt so alone, even with the doctor, nurses and techs that were all in the room.

While they were all running this way and that, I tried to imagine that I was somewhere else. Tears streamed silently out of the corners of my eyes. I had long ago learned how to do two things. Number one was how to pretend you are somewhere else. Number two is how to cry in silence.

I cannot say it was working that well today. That was a first. I felt like I could not breathe. It was as if a rock was pushing against my chest. It just felt so heavy. It was crushing me. It was preventing me from taking deep breaths. I couldn't think straight either. Of course, the blame was on me. *What had I done?*

It was then I realized that someone was speaking to me. The doctor asked me again what had happened. I cited the story as if it were a well-learned poem from my college English Literature classes. I was walking down the stairs when one of my shoes came off and I fell.

A fall could explain away a lot of bruising and other injuries in one visit. I learned that over the years. So had Jones, my husband. Since he knew that, I was sure I was up for the clumsiest patient of the year award. If I had too many injuries, I would just say that I fell. And when Jones would talk to me, mostly apologizing for what he had done, he would call it a fall as well.

"I'm so sorry about your fall. You just have to be more careful." He would say to me.

As if he wanted me to believe it. As if saying it would make it okay. I knew that he was trying to brainwash me. When he first did this, I corrected him. I reminded him that he had hit, slapped or punched me. He walked over to me, still battered and bruised and he hit me again. He then made me repeat to him that I had fallen. And that I loved him. And that I knew, how very much he loved me.

He wasn't here of course. He hardly ever came to the hospital when I was being treated for the type of love that he showed me. He would send flowers and candy to my room. That sounds sweet but I knew it was a reminder to keep my mouth shut. The textbook tactics of an abuser. I mean, it couldn't get out that the son of a high- profile Senator was beating the tar out of his wife almost daily, could it? Knowing this, he mainly stayed away.

He would then come to pick me up on discharge day looking the ever worried and loving husband. Though he was neither. As the doctor was speaking to me, my two best friends in the whole world, Tina and McKenna came rushing in. Their faces were a mix of anger and worry.

The doctor turned to greet them. They hardly responded as they gathered around my bed both hugging me and kissing me on my forehead and cheeks and rubbing my hair. They were always there to give me comfort. They were all I had now.

I talked to the doctor and told him that it was alright. He could keep speaking in front of them. They were both my next of kin, right after my husband on my records. He could tell them anything. My parents died when I was young. I had grown up in different foster homes. I had no family willing to take me in.

I had been through a lot when I met Jones. Very little of it was pleasant. We were high school and college sweethearts. He had never hit me as hard as some of the foster parents, so I thought he must love me. Neither Tina nor Kenna ever wanted me to marry him. They actually despised him. But I loved Jones. Even after everything he had done to me.

But this time it was different. He had not just hurt me. He caused me to lose our baby. '*I never listened,*' he had explained to me. I didn't even know what he was talking about. He came home from work angry. He had a stressful job day trading and he was always sure to take that out on me.

I was lying there, replaying the scene in my head. I was laying down in bed because I had not been feeling well and had been exhausted this pregnancy. But I had promised him fried fish and chips. So, I made it early. He came home and immediately started in. He was yelling in my face as per usual.

"Why is dinner cold?!?!!? Did you know it was cold?"

"Yes, because you said you would be early and that you were on your way home. That was over an hour ago. I can heat it up. It really isn't a big deal, babe." I said as I got up from the bed. He kept yelling as I put my slippers on.

"You only had one job, to take care of me and you can't even do that right."

This, of course, wasn't true. I also taught at a University. Never mind my art work that was beginning to sell really well at shows and online now. I told him I would give him a moment to calm down. As I tried to go down the steps, he grabbed me by my arm, turned me to face him and then he punched me in my face. I lost my footing and I fell backwards. He did try to grab me. As if that made it okay.

Everything went black. I awoke to him bending over me, begging me not to be dead. There was blood flowing from my head, which seemed to scare him as much as the blood that began to flow from between my legs. He said he was *sorry,* over and over. He called 911 and held the phone to my ear. I had to request the ambulance myself. He couldn't let his voice be heard, of course. He always stayed with me until he heard the sirens. He would then kiss me, tell me he was sorry and that he loved me, and then head off on his motorcycle. Or he would drop me off at the Emergency room. Like the coward that he was.

"Mrs. Rodney, we have to take you to the OR soon. We have to remove the fetus there, as the pregnancy is no longer viable. I'm so sorry." He said sincerely. I believed he was.

I just stared at him. I was in shock. And my heart was literally hurting. It was broken into pieces. I was so looking forward to having this baby. Someone to love me unconditionally. Someone I could care for. And Jones had taken that from me. Again. I realized that the doctor was speaking with me.

"Bobbi, did you understand what I've said to you? Do you understand the procedures?"

I took a second to look around the room. I took in everyone's faces, the nurses, my best friends and the doctor. I then looked on the screen of the ultrasound seeing my baby and hearing no heartbeat. She was gone. It was then I fully understood what was happening. And I screamed out loudly.

My friends held and cried with me. The doctor ordered the nurse to give me some Ativan to calm me down. He also ordered some pain medication for my broken wrist and ankle. They would fix those in surgery as well. He told me that he would come back in to check on me in a few moments. I couldn't believe what I had allowed to happen to my baby. It was one thing for Jones to hurt me, but to do this to our child. I could never forgive him.

Kenna and Tina

"I know some criminals. They would bump Jones off for less than what I charge them for an hour of work."

"Kenna, stop it. You know that's crazy talk. You know we would have to hire a hitman from out of town."

"Yes girl. Now you are talking my language. We can try in New York. I work out there sometimes. You will always find a hitman there."

"Someone with tattoos on their face. It's not like they've considered going into customer service."

"I can't believe he did this. This is too far even for Jones."

Then we noticed that the doctor was standing behind us. We immediately clammed up. He was there to tell us how Bobbi's surgery had gone. We were both wondering how much he had heard. We could tell by his face that he had heard something. He also looked kind of angry. Noticing this as well, Kenna piped in.

"Doctor Lindsay, how is she?"

It took a second before he answered. It seemed as if he wanted to say something but changed his mind.

"The surgery went very well. The Orthopedic surgeon was able to fix her ankle and her wrist. Her ankle has some screws and pins in it where the bone needed support after shattering. She says that with some physical therapy, Bobbi should be as good as new. She will also be able to conceive and have babies again. That was one of our concerns. But it was for naught."

"Thank God." Tina exhaled.

"When can we see her?" Kenna asked.

"In a little while. She is in recovery right now. We will need to give her some time to wake up and get her pain under control. After that, you ladies are free to see her."

"Thank you so much doctor. We were so worried about her. She's like our sister. We have been taking care of her, and she us, for as long as we can remember. As much as she'll let us, that is."

"I'm sure you have. With that being said, I need to ask a question so I can get with the Social worker on a discharge plan. Is there somewhere else she can go home to? I have not met her husband yet. I know she is married but she comes to her appointments alone. I would hate to release her home knowing that she is going to need a lot of help and support. Everything she had done today is what we would call major surgery. Is it possible that she would be able to stay with one of you? If not, I'm afraid I can't release her home. She would have to go to a rehabilitation center for at least a couple of weeks. I think she would be more comfortable at home."

"Absolutely. I have a condominium that she can have. And I mean she can have it. Whatever she needs, doctor. Nurses, physical therapy, you set it up and we will take care of it." Tina told him.

"Excellent." he said, with a handsome smile. "I will be releasing her within a few days as long as all goes well. She will need nurses and physical therapy, also occupational therapy too. The type of therapy that will help her with everyday things, brushing her teeth and showering, until she heals. I can set that up to come to the house that you have for her. Is there anything else you think she would need?"

"I can think of a few things." Said Kenna under her breath.

"Excuse me?" the doctor asked.

"Ignore her doctor, she speaks without thinking. If we think of anything, we will let you know. Thank you again."

He walked away and Kenna spoke..."So, New York..."

Cade

I waited as the phone just rang and rang. This was becoming a habit and I didn't think it was funny. Tina had not responded to not one call, email or text. I know that I had messed things up, royally, but damn. I honestly did not see this coming. When I was served, at the arena no less, it knocked the damn wind out of me.

In addition to this, I had called the housekeeper and had her go over and check in on Tina and the house. She told me that Tina's clothes closet, her shoe closet, her bag closet, drawers and her sink where she kept her toiletries, were all empty. She must have been planning this for a long time.

I thought she had forgiven me. I needed someone to talk to. I had to be careful who because I did not want this in the news. At least not until I figured out what this was. I grabbed my phone, sat back on the oversized couch and called my mom. Just when it rang so long that I thought she was ignoring me too, she answered sounding a little tired.

"Hey baby."

"Hey ma. You ok?"

I'm fine. I can tell you're not. What's wrong baby boy?" she asked me. Genuinely concerned.

"What makes you think there is something wrong?"

"I know both of you like the back of my hand. I also know how my babies sound when something is pressing on them. Tell me what it is."

"Ma, Tutu is leaving me. I was just served with separation papers. She moved out and she won't take my calls."

"Uh huh." She responded.

"Ma. That's all you have to say? You don't sound surprised."

"No. I have plenty to say. I'm not surprised that she is leaving. I am, however, surprised that you did not see this coming from ten miles away. I mean, just how long did you think that girl was going to put up with you and your foolery, Caden?"

"Put up with me?" I asked. Surprised to hear her saying what she was.

"Boy, don't you dare play stupid. You have been running around on that child since you signed that first contract. You all up on TMZ caught out with some random in your lap in a club one day, then dragging that girl all across the red carpet as if you haven't just embarrassed her. You ought to be ashamed of yourself. I know I didn't raise you like that, that's what I know."

"Mama. You supposed to be on my side."

"I am. I always have been, and I always will be on your side. But I don't co-sign no foolishness or entertain the ridiculous. Both my children know that as pure fact."

"Oh, I know..."

"She put up with more than I would have. I will tell you that right now. Your daddy tried that on me once. He woke up with my switchblade to his neck. I told him if he ever cheated on me again, he better never let me find out about it. Not even years later or the next time he was gonna wake up at the pearly gates."

I sat straight up at that.

"Mama. No, you didn't..."

"Call him right now and ask him. He out playing golf. He'd better be, in any case. I have that switchblade until this day."

"Well, ain't this some stuff."

"Maybe I will give it to my daughter-in-law for a birthday present."

"MAMA!!!!!"

"What?!?" she asked as if she hadn't just told me would assist my wife in my demise.

"You can take the girl out of North Philly but you can't take the North Philly out of the girl. Okay thug life, what should I do to get her back?"

"Nothing."

"Nothing??"

"Yes. Nothing for now. She needs time. Give it to her. She's hurting. You caused it. She don't want to talk to you. If you keep on calling her and bothering her, she will run faster and farther away. Maybe into the arms of someone else."

"Ma! Don't say that. She wouldn't start seeing someone else. Do you really think she would?"

Now I was legit scared. I had not even thought of her being with someone else. I had only been thinking of her *NOT* being with me. Damn. I felt like my mom had just delivered the gut punch that only she could. She had a name for it too. The truth.

"Why not? You did it with no separation papers. And she not homely looking either. She's a, what do the kids call it? Dessert..."

"Are you trying to call my wife a snack, mom? I said with an unbelieving smile on my face. She was too funny.

"Yeah! That's it, a snack. And men are always hungry. You gonna have to give that girl her space. Let her find some peace."

"What if she forgets about me or she decides she don't want me back?"

"Oh, I doubt she will ever forget what you did to her. And if she does decide that it is over then you have to respect it. In the meantime, I suggest you do some work on you."

"Now what does that mean?"

"Show her that you want to change, Tiger Woods. Get a therapist. Stay out the blogs with these little hot thangs in your face. She should only see you making baskets and going home."

"You're right, ma."

"I know. But look here, I love you. Your daddy does too. We are very proud of you. No one is perfect. You got caught up in the lifestyle. But it comes with consequences. You know what you have to do now."

"Yes ma'am...I love you guys too."

"Alright, well I'm headed to go teach my knitting class to the seniors at the center where I volunteer. I'll call and check in on you later."

After we hung up, I just sat there thinking. She was right. I had brought this mess on myself. I had never thought about how embarrassing it was for her to show up with me to events when these rumors, some false but mostly true, were floating around. I had been selfish and arrogant. I can promise this, I am definitely feeling humbled.

I was going to do everything that my mom said. First though, I needed to try and call her one more time. Because my mom was right, she was a snack. She was a whole meal, actually. Yeah, I'm calling. Two times at the most. No more than three, I promised myself. I mean, sometimes it is in her bag and she can't get to it. I said making up excuses that she didn't need. After that I would go to sleep.....probably.

Tina

I wished Caden would stop calling. Now he's super concerned about our marriage, he didn't seem that concerned when he had Kimber's thongs in his mouth. And yes, he really had an affair with a girl named Kimber. He's calling my friends, my sisters, my mom, and my dad. My dad told him to bite it. I am his baby girl after all.

It has been almost three months since he had gotten the separation papers. Lawrence did not play. He and I have become good friends as well. I felt no remorse for leaving and staying gone. It took me a while to get to this place. Usually I would take Cade back after about a week of giving him the cold shoulder. Now, I genuinely did not want to speak to him. I also could do without seeing his face. I would say this, he hadn't made the blogs for anything shady lately.

However, I did like basketball. Meaning I would catch the games. I would also root for him and his team. I had been a fan of them since I was a girl. Him being drafted there was pure coincidence. Other than that, as far as I was concerned, our marriage was over.

He had damaged it beyond repair. I'm not saying I was perfect, but I never had an affair, or even entertained any other men. I hadn't even slept with him for at least five months before the separation papers. I just was not attracted to the man that he had become. He thought that it was because he was traveling for games.

I needed to be stimulated outside the bedroom before we could take it inside. He knew this about me, but he stopped trying as well. It wasn't as if it mattered to him. He had a plethora of girls ready and willing to take him to bed. Probably doing things I had never heard of. See, I was a virgin when we met. He had basically taught me what he liked in the bedroom. These chicks came with experience that I probably didn't have.

That's not to say the sex was bad. He seemed to love it. Or that I wasn't open to trying new things. I absolutely was. So, I had allowed him to teach me. He was my husband after all. I always wanted to satisfy him. But he made me begin to feel insecure with all of the affairs. I still kept trying. I went to classes on oral sex, bought books and tried to keep it spicy for both of us. I mean, I needed satisfaction too.

Well, all of that is in the past now. We could talk through lawyers from now on. Though I can't imagine what there is left to say. Lawrence has already told him what I want from him. I am entitled to half, and he knows it. That's probably another reason he wants to work it out. *$15 million* is a lot of money to lose. Well, I guess he should have thought of that. He was probably kicking himself right now.

He should be thanking God I didn't want any of the joint property we owned. He could sell it, move all his girls in Hugh Hefner style, whatever would float his boat. The other day, I had received a message from Lawrence. He had heard back from Cade's lawyer and wanted to talk.

We were meeting at a sushi bar. There was nothing better than a spicy tuna roll with yum yum sauce and a glass of Pinot. I ordered one glass and sipped on it as I waited on him to arrive. I looked around, just people watching. Then my phone rang. "Cade" popped up. I kindly slid the red decline button over to his name. Not today buddy.

After about ten minutes, he came strolling through the door. He was dressed in a button up shirt with the sleeves rolled up. It was a hot day, after all. I could tell he spent a fair amount of time in the gym. His freshly twisted dreads hung loose about his shoulders. He reminded me of a lion on the prowl as he scanned the restaurant for me. I snapped out of it and raised my hand so that he would see me.

He headed over with a smile that revealed perfectly white teeth. My goodness. Is there anything better than a black man with white teeth? I can't think of one. He kissed me on the cheek before he spoke. That sent a shiver through me that I don't remember ever feeling before. It shocked the hell out of me.

"Hey, Tina. I'm sorry I was late. I was sitting in my car outside negotiating a settlement offer for a client. Please forgive me?" He said with just the hint of a question in his voice. He had better stop teasing me.

"No worries. I have nowhere to be."

"Have you ordered?"

"Just a glass of wine. I wasn't sure what you'd want...."

"Say no more. You are my last meeting of the day. Do you mind if I order a Coor's light with my sushi."

"Absolutely not. I actually hate drinking alone."

"Then we should have a round of warm sake too." He suggested with a smile. Just then the waiter arrived to take our orders.

"I'll have the spicy tuna..."

"That's my favorite..." he said before I finished.

"Really? I asked with a smile."

He then turned to the waiter.

"Bring that, warm sake...and tell the chef to surprise us with something else good." He said. After the waiter left, he turned to me. "I hope you like surprises."

"Absolutely..."

We both smiled at each other for a few moments. I then started to blush and looked away. Taking a sip of my water and then of my wine. I felt I needed to break the silence.

"So, you said we heard from Cade's attorney?"

"Ahh...yes. I'm sorry. I was distracted." He said with a smile. "His attorney states that your husband would like to attend marriage counseling with you. They wanted to know if you are amenable to that."

"Oh please. Now he wants counseling. I have been suggesting it for years. He actually did show up to two sessions after the fourth affair. He then decided that we were fine and stopped coming."

"After only two sessions?"

"Two..."

"Wow. I imagine that I am telling him no?"

"Tell him, hell no. Though he should invest in it himself."

"I'd agree that anyone who would cheat on such a beautiful woman definitely needs therapy."

I blushed again and turned away. I had never blushed before. This was crazy. He saw this and smiled.

"I'm sorry. I made you blush. And as cute as that is. That was out of line and unprofessional."

"No. It's fine. I won't tell if you don't."

"I can keep a secret. I am actually bound by law to keep yours." He told me.

"Really? Then here's one. I haven't been called beautiful in years. Not to my face anyway."

He sat back in his chair, took a sip of his beer and studied me. He then leaned back up and spoke.

"I can see that. Because beautiful actually doesn't do you justice."

There I was, blushing again. Just then the waiter came out with our food and sake. Lawrence ordered another beer and glass of wine for me. We talked for hours. We drifted back and forth between my case and getting to know each other on a personal level. We had so much in common. From our love of history and reading to our taste in music. He was even surprised I could quote basketball stats.

Neither of us wanted the evening to end. At least that was the energy I was getting from him. Good thing the restaurant was in Town Center. There were bars, restaurants, high end shops and clubs all within walking distance. We walked to a Spanish club and danced the salsa and meringue...badly. We blamed it on the Sake. But we laughed the whole time and had so much fun.

No matter how fast or slow the song, he kept me pressed against him. And I found I liked it and didn't want him to let go. Three shots of 1800 and a long island later, we found ourselves across the street from the club, at the Marriott.

We didn't even wait to make it to our suite. By the time we were in the elevator, we were already locked in the most passionate kiss I had ever experienced, at least that I could recall. I knew from the way he looked at me, and the way he held me when we kissed, that he longed for me. Burned for me even. And I did for him too.

We were barely through the door of the suite before clothing was being ripped off. We left a trail to the bed like a movie. He took his shirt off, with my help, and then undid my shorts. I kicked my heels off and he did the same with his shoes. I kissed from his chest down to his stomach, which I'm pretty sure is the picture in the dictionary next to six-pack. I then did it in reverse and found his lips again. My shirt and bra were the next to go. Where they went, I had no clue.

The next thing I knew, we were standing a few feet from the bed, both naked. I used my hands to cover myself. He took them, kissed them both and gently guided them down to my side. He stepped back and whispered...

"You have no need to hide yourself away. I need to take you in."

With that he used his finger to trace my body. Starting with my face. He then moved in closer to begin to kiss me everywhere his finger had traveled. I began to feel nervous and butterflies. As he kissed my stomach, I ran my fingers through his dreads. My head tilted back leaving my face looking towards the heavens as I enjoyed being explored.

"Lawrence.."

"Larry..." he corrected me, without stopping.

"Larry...you should know something..." I whispered.

He brought his head back up and faced me. The look on his face was so intense. It caused me to become more nervous.

"What is that?"

"I'm so embarrassed to even say it. I've only ever been with my husband. And the last time was months ago, close to a year..." I admitted.

I could see his face change. He touched his forehead to mine and pulled me into him.

"I knew you were special. There is no pressure. We can just watch a movie and go to bed. Netflix and chill, but for real." He said with a smile before he kissed my forehead.

I thought for a moment. Then I kissed him as deeply as he had done me. I then whispered to him...

"...no...keep going...."

"Are you sure? he asked.

I nodded my head yes. With that, he lifted me from my feet with one strong arm. I wrapped my legs around his waist and he carried me the remainder of the way to the bed.

"Lie back. Let me do all of the work." he said. I did as I was told.

He kissed my whole body. Every blemish and every curve. He even tended to my feet. From there he gently opened my legs, and placed his face between them, and went to work. I moaned and screamed his name, and other words, out in pleasure, which seemed to encourage him to do more. Cade had some things to learn it seemed to me.

Larry did not stop until it was obvious to us both that I had been pleasured...more than once. He then came up to look me directly in my eyes.

"Are you ready?"

Still shaking, I nodded yes. He then slowly entered me. I could hear him cuss, several times, under his breath. I dug my nails into his arms and chest and yelled out. It felt like my first time. I could tell he fought the urge to finish until I was, once again, satisfied. As I reached my peak, he joined me, loudly. He was unable to hold out any longer. He then collapsed on top of me.

"Shit babe..." he said into my neck, where his face was buried. I lie there...speechless. We continued to make love for hours after that. With short breaks in between until we literally could not keep our eyes open. I awoke to my phone alarm ringing at eight thirty. I reached over and turned it off as quickly as I could so that it didn't wake him. He had slept holding me so tightly, I could barely move to go to the bathroom during the night. And I didn't do anything to stop him.

I slid from under his arms and headed to the bathroom to shower. I had to pick Bobbi up by *1030* and take her to her follow-up with the surgeons. And I still needed to go home and change my clothes. As I stood under the hot water, allowing it to soothe the soreness in my body, Lawrence slid into the shower behind me. He took the washcloth from me and began kissing and washing my neck and back. I did the same for him.

"You're amazing. Last night was amazing..."

"Yeah, but I'm paying for it today." I joked.

"I'm sorry, I would never want to hurt you. I had no idea you were... I mean...that you only had one lover." he said as he looked in my eyes with sincerity.

"You have nothing to apologize for." I assured him with a kiss.

"I wish you didn't have to go." He said as we stood facing each other. Allowing the hot water to bead down over us.

I was thinking the same thing. But something stopped me from saying it. I just nodded and lay my head on his chest. What was I doing? Even though I was separated, I was still married. And he was my lawyer. Talk about blurred lines. After a few moments, there was a knock on the door. It startled me.

"Maybe it's the people next door. You were kind of loud last night." I said with shoulder shrug.

"Oh, I was the loud one? You re-writing history already." He said smiling and showing those teeth again as he sat the soap down.

"I ordered you breakfast...and an outfit from the Gucci store around the corner. I represent the owner. We go way back and she's always there super early. It is probably either one of those." he said, hopping out the shower and wrapping a towel around his waist.

I couldn't believe him. But sure enough, when I came out of the bathroom, there were egg white omelettes, turkey sausage, wheat toast with strawberry jelly and a purple shorts romper, size 8, awaiting me. Even a new bra and panty set. Gucci as well. I mean, the man did pay attention. He got my favorite breakfast, size and favorite color of clothing right.

"You did all this for me. Why?" I asked.

"I told you last night. I like you, you're special. And I love spending time with you. And you deserve to be treated like a queen."

He had saved me at least an hour since I didn't need to go home for clothes. To me, that meant I might as well spend it wisely. With that, I let the towel I was wrapped in drop to the floor, and then I thanked him, properly.

Bobbi and Tina

I sat in the passenger side of Tina's purple beamer, head back and gazing out the window. I had been depressed and angry since I had lost the baby. Jones had come up to the hospital the day after I had the surgeries. I wasn't expecting that at all. I should have had him arrested on the spot. I didn't have the heart. I never did.

Dr. Lindsay came in several times to check on me. Especially when he saw Jones sitting by the bed. I was pretty sure he was shooting daggers from his eyes at him, almost as if he knew what had really happened. But I was obviously imagining it. I was on heavy pain and anxiety meds and strong antibiotics after all. I knew no one had told him the truth. But still, I almost felt like he was there to protect me.

Jones seemed so remorseful this time. He even shed a tear or two when the doctor explained to him that I had suffered a miscarriage and everything that he had to do in the OR to be sure I could conceive again. I was not so easily moved this time by his performance. I barely even spoke to him. He brought my favorite flowers everyday that I was there. I was less than impressed.

Dr. Lindsay had spoken to Tina and Kenna about me having somewhere to stay as I was rehabbing. When Jones heard that I actually was not coming home with him, he was beyond livid. He was even more upset when I told him I wasn't sure where I was going. Tina had a home for me. We both knew she had property all over the state. This could be anywhere. He also knew that she borderline hated him. He didn't put her keeping where I would be a secret beyond her. Not even from me. Just in case I slipped up and told him.

They had gone by the house when he was at work and packed my clothes and art studio up. And they were very happy to do so. Dr. Lindsay told him I would be released on Thursday. On Wednesday morning, as I sat in the chair by the window, gazing out and thinking, he came in my room and announced I was being discharged a day early. I'm pretty sure he planned this slight of hand.

I did not call my husband. This was surprising. Even to me. I called my friends and they both dropped what they were doing and came to pick me up. I loved these girls so much. They were there through everything. They cried with me. Took me to my appointments every week. They were there every step of the way as I healed. They were encouraging me through therapy and watching the nurses like hawks.

Dr. Lindsay called to check on me almost everyday. He had even made a couple of house calls to check on my progress. I didn't even know doctors still did that. Now, today was the day. I was headed to my last appointment. At least I hoped it was the last one. That all depended on how everything looked on the x-rays and scans. I had been healing well and couldn't wait to get back to my life. Whatever that was now.

I turned to look at Tina. As she drove, she was dancing and singing along to Amerie's "One thing" song. I watched her for at least a minute. When she started singing "OooOoo" I had to intervene.

"Umm...spill it chica.."

"Spill what?" She asked innocently.

"I know you. You're dancing and frikking glowing. Spill it."

"There's nothing to spill...."

"You are thee worst liar. I'm calling Kenna." I threatened, picking up my phone. She never could stand up under her cross examination.

"No!!!...and look. There's no time anyway. We're here." She said with a smirk as we pulled into the parking lot of his private practice.

"Ok. Fine. But you better be ready to share at girl's night tonight, or you are definitely going on the stand."

We both laughed at that. Not long after arriving, I was sent to ultrasound and X-Ray. He had everything there. It was like a mini hospital. After those test were complete, I was then shown into his private office. I thought I would be in a cold examine room. That was not the case, thank goodness. It was such a nice office, I thought as I looked around. There was music playing softly. I started singing along.

"*Oo...smokestack lightning...where did you, stay last night, oh don't you hear me crying...ooo...*"

I was so into the song, I didn't hear him come in behind me. I didn't know he was there until he spoke.

"What you know about Howling wolf?" He asked as he walked over to sit in the chair next to me instead of behind his desk.

"More than you I bet." I answered.

This made him laugh out loud.

"What's so funny?" I asked.

"Nothing. I just didn't take you for a blue's lover."

"Oh, I'm sorry, are you a doctor or a lawyer. Since you're judging books by their covers..." I teased him.

"You're right. I did. I'm sorry. So, you like the blues?"

"And rock, and jazz. I paint to jazz on occasion. It calms me."

"Wow, you're an artist too. I love art. I'd love to see some of your pieces someday."

"Well, as a matter of fact, I have an art show coming up downtown. It's next month. I had to postpone it, since my accident and everything..."

"Of course. Well, I would love to come."

"You would?"

"You ask as if that's hard to believe."

"I'm sorry. I guess it surprised me. My husband never comes. He thinks it's a waste of time."

I thought I saw a flash of anger mixed with annoyance, fly across his face.

"I'd wager you've wasted plenty of time on things, but I doubt art is one of them."

He stared at me for a few moments. I, all of a sudden, started feeling very self-conscious, so I changed the subject.

Speaking of art shows, I need my wrist to finish some pieces. How does it look? Good I hope."

"Right. I'm sorry. Yes, results. Your wrist and ankle have healed nicely according to ortho. you will need to finish out the last couple of therapy sessions. But they say you're doing great as well."

"And the other?" I asked. Talking about my miscarriage.

"The ultrasound looks good. No scar tissue and no free fluid. You are free to start trying again, if you'd like."

I don't think so. Not right now, at least. I have some decisions to make before I do that. Even though I wanted my baby...so much..." I trailed off as tears sprung to my eyes.

He jumped from his chair and knelt in front of me. Pulling a tissue from the box on his desk and began dabbing my tears with it. "I'm sorry you had to suffer such a loss. It's hard I know." He said in a voice that was full of caring and sadness.

"Thank you..." I said, as we again, caught each other's eyes.

Just then, a voice came through the phone on his desk. It was his front desk secretary. "*Dr. Lindsay. Your 12 and 12:30 appointments just walked in.*"

"Thanks Lorie. I'm wrapping up now."

Even though he spoke to her, he never took his eyes off of me. It actually gave me chills.

"Well. I don't want to take up anymore of your time, doctor."

"No. You're important. I mean, all my patients are, of course." He said after he realized what he had said.

He stood up, took one of his cards, flipped it over and wrote on the back. He then handed it to me.

"Here's my cell. Don't forget to call me about the art show. I wouldn't want to miss it, or you. And if you need anything, anything at all. Even if it's a question in the middle of the night. Call me."

"..ok..." I said, shocked.

With that we both left his office. He walked me to the front, made small talk with Tina and I for a minute and then headed to see his next appt. When we were in the car, Tina looked over and saw his card in my hand. She snatched it and read it.

"Ummm...is this Dr. Sexy's cell number?" She asked.

"Yes. He wants me to send him the info about my art show."

"Ummm hmmm...he must also want you to call him Kelvin..."

"Huh?" I asked.

She flipped the card over so that I could see it. And as sure as she was glowing and singing on the way here, he had written his first name, his personal cell number and "CALL ANYTIME!" On the card.

"What exactly were you two doing back there?" She asked teasingly.

"I'll tell you, after you tell me why you're lit up like a Christmas tree."

"Any who. You hungry? Cause I'm hungry....."

Jones

I was in my office pacing back and forth. My secretary was directed to hold all of my calls. Unless it was Bobbi. *Where in the hell was my wife anyway?* That's what I wanted to know. I was coming unglued. I wasn't into having her try to teach me any lessons. She knew that for sure.

I was not one of her unwashed art students. Where would that take them anyway? Nowhere. Was she talented? I guess so. But, she could do so much more if she was would just listen to me. With her hard- headed ass. See, I never wanted to hit her. She makes me do it with her smart mouth and dreams. Why couldn't she just be happy by my side. Like my parents. WHERE WAS SHE???!!!....

A knock on my door disrupted my thoughts and stopped me in my tracks. A few seconds later, my sister Jasmine and brother Jackson walked in. They never waited for me to answer their knocks. Jazz went right over and closed the blinds that allowed our company's employees to look into our office. Even more important, we were able to watch them. Dad was big on us knowing their comings and goings.

"What is going on with you, Jones?" My brother asked.

"Did you sleep here?" Jazz asked as she looked at the blanket and pillow thrown in the corner of my office couch.

"Yeah. Why?"

"Were you in a late negotiation or something?"

"No. It's Bobbi."

"How is she feeling? You know, after everything." Jazz asked me.

"I don't have a clue." I snapped.

"Chill out and tell us what's going on." Jackson said, sitting in the chair on the other side of my desk.

"She didn't come home after she was discharged. When I got to the hospital, they told me that she was let go a day earlier. I knew she hadn't been home, because I was there. I checked my phone thinking that I had missed her calls to pick her up somehow. Nothing."

"Nothing?" Jazz asked.

"That's what I said." I said pointedly.

"Jones. What exactly happened that caused her to lose the baby?" Jack asked me in his holier than thou tone of voice.

"I told you, she fell down the stairs..."

"Yes, but how?" Jazz followed up.

"What do you mean, how. I don't know. She just fell."

"Did you push that girl down the stairs? Or do anything to cause it?" Jazz asked. Abandoning any etiquette or decorum.

"Why are you grilling me? You don't believe me?" I argued.

"No. I, for one, do not believe you. Why would she just disappear into the night after being released from the hospital if you did nothing to put her there? It doesn't make any sense." Jackson deduced.

I sat there seething, but not answering either of them.

"Oh, my goodness, Jones. You didn't. That was your first child. I can't believe you." Jazz yelled.

"It was an accident Jazzy. I promise. I was upset and we argued near the top of the stairs..."

"Uugghh...I can't even look at you right now. You are worse than dad." She said as she flew over to open the door.

"That's not fair.." I whined.

"No. It's not. For her and my poor niece that we'll never meet. I personally hope she never comes back to you." she spit out with venom I had never heard from her.

With that she threw the door open and almost ran out. Jackson wasn't done with me. After that episode he stood, closed the door behind her and sat back down.

"You going to yell at me too?"

"Nope. It won't help. Apparently beating your ass doesn't do anything either. I tried that the first time I found bruises on her. This time, I'll talk to you. Man to man, as it were. You need help."

"I know."

"Yeah? Do you really know? Because I think that if you did know, you would be trying to get it."

"Well, what. Is there like, a support group for men who manhandle their wives a little bit?"

"First of all, you need to come out of denial. You don't manhandle your wife a little bit. You beat your wife. You are an abuser. Just like dad. If you don't know where to start, try anger management. If you don't do anything to help yourself, then you don't deserve her. Or any other woman."

"It's so easy for you to judge me. You think I want to be like this?" I asked.

"I don't know. I honestly don't. But if you didn't, I have to believe you would try to do something about it. Until then, I'm with Jazz. I hope she stays far away from you. Before you kill her, like you did your baby. If that doesn't send you begging for help, nothing will."

All I could do was nod my head. He was right. He usually was. My big level-headed brother. We grew up seeing the same things. Mom hiding her bruises that dad gave her when he was upset. I remembered being so mad at dad.

Why then, was I just like him? I didn't want to be. And why wasn't Jackson?

"Jones! I mean it."

"I know. I hear you Jack. I am going to get help. I promise. First though, I have to find my wife."

"You haven't heard a word we've said. Have you?"

"Yes. I have."

"Look. Go home. Take a shower and get some sleep. I don't want to see you back here until you have found a therapist or anger management group. Something. Do you understand?"

"Oh, are you pulling rank?" I asked.

"Yes. I am. Technically, I am your boss. Even here in dad's company. Now go. It's for your own good."

"Fine. I'm going."

"I'll call you later and check in on you." he added.

"Ok..." I said as I packed my work bag and grabbed my suit jacket and tie.

As I walked by him, he grabbed my arm and pulled me in for a hug. I returned it. We walked out to the elevators together. As soon as I stepped off of the elevator and in the lobby, I pulled my phone out again. Checking for a missed call. As if she had reached out in the one place that I didn't get reception, the elevator. I needed to find my wife. She couldn't leave me like this. I wouldn't allow it.

Kenna

"Kenna, Jeff is here, should I send him in?" Miracle asked standing in my door.

"Yes. Thank you." I said without even looking up.

I had briefs that I needed to look at. Namely, concerning the case Jeff was here to discuss. A few seconds later he walked in. Looking like Idris Elba's little brother. This came with the accent. He moved to the United States from the UK after graduating Oxford two years early. He came here to attend Law school at Fordham, in New York. Which was my Alma mater. Good grief, everytime I saw him I had to tell myself to focus. And not on him.

"Hello counselor. Are you and your client ready to settle? We'd be absolutely chuffed to bits to hear it." He asked as he took a seat and laid his satchel on my desk and retrieved papers from it.

"Now why would we do that when your client was obviously at fault? As a matter of fact, if that's a check from your client that you're holding there, we can all head home for an early weekend."

"You'd love that bit there wouldn't you then? Sorry to disappoint you, but it's going to take a bit more than you batting those pretty brown eyes there at me to get us to admit fault."

I laughed as I leaned back in my chair. He studied me as if I was question number three on the bar examine. His face went from light hearted banter to the face he wore when he entered the courtroom and began winning. Which he did almost as much as I did these days.

"How are you getting on there, darling?" He asked.

"Fine...."

"If I didn't know you, I'd actually believe that. " he said as he stood and came over to me, grabbed my hand and led me over to the couch.

"Come here then. Share your miseries with your mate." He encouraged me.

"I hate to complain. But, since you asked, I have my two best paralegals out. One has a sick grandmother in another state and the other is on maternity leave. Which I'm just realizing I'll probably never have. The paralegals from the temp agency are little to no help. And I'm being generous. I'm not even sure that one of them can read. Then there's Tina, who is in the middle of a divorce. Then there is Bobbi, who is still healing after her husband basically beat our godchild out of her, breaking her wrist AND ankle in the process." I stopped speaking when I realized I had my head on his shoulder and he was dabbing the tears from my eyes with his Armstrong and Wilson pocket square.

I was expecting some generic advice. Especially from him. Mainly because men didn't listen. Not to mention, he was about two or three years younger than me. Which may as well be dog years between men and women. But he happened to actually surprise me.

"Ok, firstly...throw those paralegals back. I'll send Maura over on Monday...."

"Oh...I love Maura..." I gushed.

"Also...fyi, you don't have to try every case. Look around darling, you have a corner office. A partner's office, delegate. We've talked about this before, haven't we then?"

"I know, but I'm the only African-American female partner. I have too much to prove. If I sit back and assign all my cases to junior partners and lawyers like Ted, Hank and Liam do, I'll be called lazy."

"I agree. But you're not going to retire and take up golf. You're going to delegate. Keep the ones you're passionate about. Kick the others to your team. Give the newbies a chance. It's how we learned, yeah?"

"Yeah...makes sense..." I admitted.

"How are Tina and Caden getting on with the divorce then?"

"She's gongho. Lawrence is handling her side."

"Larry's the black hulk. All he hears is "smash" when the gavel hits, doesn't he?"

"Exactly why I introduced them. Caden is not handling it well, though."

"Well nothing teaches a cheating bastard to keep it in his pants quicker than giving up half I'd wager."

We both laughed at that. I thought that was it, but I was wrong. He kept going.

"So then, I have got some friends in New York with face tattoos and colored handkerchiefs. Not to mention some proper Welsh thugs who'd love cracking heads. I am telling you darling, these lads would love nothing more than a trip across the pond to do it. I'm just putting that out there, darling. The world would be a better place..."

I burst out laughing. I told him that Tina and I had the EXACT same conversation about Jones. I needed that laugh. We joked about it for a few more moments. I then stood up to look in the mirror in my bathroom and fix my make-up. He stood leaning against the door frame, watching me.

"One more thing there, Kenna.."

"What's up?" I asked as I broke open the Fenty.

"Someday...soon, I'd wager, some bloak will realize how special you are. A fact I am quite well aware of. You will let him in. He will love you the way you deserve. He will run you to the altar, and soon after, you will have your maternity leave. And those children will be geniuses and more than easy on the eyes won't they? because their mum is."

I stopped contouring and turned to look at him. In that moment, I saw him as more than a colleague and friend. The butterflies I hadn't felt in years came back to think that someone thought I was worthy of my dreams.

"Do you really think so?"

"I'm as sure of that as I am that you're going down on this case, you cheeky minx.." he said with a smile.

"Oh. Then it was all just wishful thinking..." I teased him.

We both laughed at that.

"Let me take you out tonight." He said.

I turned and leaned against the sink to think. I was about two seconds from accepting his offer when I remembered that I already had plans.

"Not tonight..."

"What is it you Americans say? .Ahh yes...He swings..."

"..no..listen. Only because this is our girl's night out. And you can imagine how much we need it with their drama and my emotional meltdown... which you singlehandedly resolved, might I add."

"Right. Yeah .I'd agree with that. Ok. Tomorrow then. We're gonna dress up in dashikis and go see Black Panther. You haven't been yet, have you?"

"..No. I've been so busy, but I want to see it badly." I told him.

He pulled out his phone and bought tickets as we stood in the doorway of my office bathroom.

"Alright. The movie is at 6:26 tomorrow night. We're going in looking like citizens of Wakanda. After, we are going to the first Indian restaurant we come to. Next, we are going to find a Spanish club or one having a Reggae night and dance the night away. Tomorrow, my lady, I'm gonna show you the world..."

All I could do was laugh.

"Tomorrow then...." I said.

With that, he gave me the hug I sorely needed. I actually didn't want to let go. When we finally released each other from the embrace, he grabbed his briefcase and walked to the door of my office.

"..oh, and my client wants his lawyer's fees paid as well. And we both know that I am wildly expensive..."

With that he disappeared and I stood there, looking forward to our date. I hadn't had that feeling in years..."Tomorrow then." I said under my breath...

The Girls

"There she is." Bobbi said as Kenna ran in.

"Hey y'all!!!" she said, kissing us both on the cheek. "Did you order my margaritas?"

"But of course." Tina said.

"Now ladies, what's the tea?" Kenna asked.

Bobbi cleared her throat and turned in Tina's direction.

"Don't look over here at me, Bobbi." Tina said with a sly smirk on her face.

"Take your own advice, Tina." Bobbi said.

"What in the world did you two get into? I left you alone for one afternoon and look at the two of you. Spill. The. Tea." Kenna said, clapping her hand to each word for maximum effect.

"Tina was extra glowy and happy this morning. Twist out on Yass!! Melanin poppin and bopping around and singing Amerie. Stereo pumping like when we were teenagers trying to get attention. And she won't say why." Bobbi said like a sibling telling on her sister to their mom and dad.

They both looked at Tina, Kenna with her arms crossed. But she just sipped her pinot and stared back.

"Must I put you on the stand, Tina?"

"Sure, but, remember I can invoke my fifth amendment rights."

"Sorry boop, only in a free country. THIS is bestie land, you have no rights."

We all laughed at this. All of a sudden, Kenna stopped laughing.

"Bobbi, when did you say this glow started?"

"She has been glowing all day. When she came to pick me up, I wasn't sure if it was her or Mr. sun driving.."

"Thank you, ma'am. You have been a helpful witness."

"Tina, did you not have a meeting with Lawrence yesterday concerning your divorce?"

"That is correct."

"And when did this said meeting end?" Kenna asked with a straight face.

"Well, now that is hard to say. I didn't exactly time it. I can try to text him and ask him about the billable hours." I said in a professional voice.

"Objection!" Bobbi half yelled.

"On what grounds? Tina asked.

"Because witness is being a smart ass." Bobbi said with a smirk.

"I plead the fifth." Tina said.

"The fifth is not recognized here. We established that earlier. Please answer the question. Or be held in contempt." Kenna said holding back her laugh.

"Fine. Nosy Nancy and Tattling Teresa. The meeting ended, If I had to guess, I mean if I was really pressed to say....it was probably, give or take about 30 minutes before I picked Bobbi up for her appointment." Tina admitted before taking a big sip of her wine.

"I knew it! You were waaaay too happy this morning." Said Bobbi.

"You didn't!" Said Kenna.

"So. What one thing did he do, Amerie?" Bobbi teased.

"What one thing did he not do would be easier to answer. The other would have us here way passed our bedtimes." Tina answered as they both laughed.

"Tina! He is your lawyer. You can not have a relationship with him."

"Well good. Because we are not in a relationship."

"Then what would you call it?" Kenna asked.

"Having a little fun. We had a few drinks, headed to Juan's, danced...drank some more...then ended up at the Marriott."

"I can't believe you."

"What is the big deal?"

"Ok, A is conflict of interest. B. You're married..." Kenna said.

"Technically, they're separated." Bobbi chimed in.

"What she said." Tina added as she and Bobbi started laughing. Forcing a smile to spread across Kenna's face.

"I just want you to be careful. It could be considered a conflict of interest. And if Cade finds out.."

"...Then good on him." Tina interjected.

"..just be careful, please?" Kenna said with a sigh.

"I will babe. It's all good. Speaking of my exploits. What about Kelvin?" Tina asked as she turned to stare at Bobbi.

"Geez...Bobbi. you too? Is everyone getting their groove back but me??" Kenna whined.

"Oh please. I'm hardly doing any grooving. I am not even rocking slowly back and forth." Bobbi said.

"All I know is she practically spent all day in Dr. Lindsay's office. After he walked her out, she had a card with his FIRST name and instructions to call him, ANYTIME." Tina said.

"He's my doctor."

Tina and Kenna looked at each other, smiled, and then both started singing...

"Mama, mama, I feel sick, call the doctor..quick, quick, quick..."

Bobbi looked around, embarrassed and whispered "Stop it. Ya'll crazy."

They all started laughing.

"He just wants to come to my art show."

"Or be your nude model. Either way...YASSS girl." Kenna said while snapping her fingers. The whole table then erupted into laughter again.

As the laughter died down, Tina looked over at Kenna.

"So how are you feeling? You sounded overwhelmed when I called you earlier. What's up?"

"Girl I was. Too much to even get into right now. Maybe later. I might start to cry to even think about it. But It's all good now. I have my girls with me. Also, Jeff is sending me some help next week. So that's a plus. And hey, before I forget, Tina, I need you to two-strand twist me tonight. I need a banging twist out for the movie tomorrow."

"Umm...what am I missing? Did we say we were going to a movie and I forgot?" Tina asked.

"Maybe all that headboard banging knocked it out your...."Bobbi started before receiving a glare from Tina that caused her to stop speaking in mode sentence and everyone to laugh again.

"No chica. Jeff and I are headed out to see Blank Panther tomorrow. He wants to dress in African garb and go all out. He's so crazy."

 She looked up to see her friends staring at her in surprise.

"Jeff, that dish of a lawyer that you introduced us to at that dinner?" Tina asked.

"Didn't you say you don't date lawyers?" Bobbi added.

"It's not a date. I was super-stressed today. He came by to negotiate the case we are working on. He listened to my rant, and said, let's go see a movie..."

"Kenna, issa date boo.." Bobbi said.

They all burst out in laughter again.

"We are just friends. It's a freate."

"Now she is in here making up words. I just can't deal with her." Tina said.

"Well, I'm pretty sure it won't end in a suite at the Marriott..."

"Only because the theatre is closer to the Sheraton..." Tina shot back without missing a beat.

We laughed again as Bobbi ordered another round of drinks. Girls night was in full swing.

Caden

"Cade, what the hell? If you keep playing like this we're gonna have a trash ass season. Where has your mind been the last couple of months?" Khalil asked.

"Man, she still not taking my calls, dawg."

"Who, Tee?"

"Everything I had my lawyer bring to her, she's shooting it down."

"Did you try diamonds? Chicks love a little bling dog."

"Did I try diamonds? Of course, I tried diamonds. I sent her a ring that made Kobe look like he got his wife's apology ring from a gumball machine. Everything I send her she has sent back via messenger. She doesn't even include a note. A messenger shows up. Tells me he needs me to sign and he hands me my gifts back, unopened."

"What about therapy? They love doing that."

"Nope. And I quote, "hell no". At least that's the response that her lawyer gave to mine."

"Damn dog. I'm sorry to hear that. But that's what happens when we get caught up in this game life. Females everywhere, we get weak. And they get fed up. And the smart ones like Tee, are educated and have their own money. They're not waiting around for us to get finished playing the field anymore."

"Man, facts. But I want my wife back. I can't help it."

"I don't blame you. She's a stunner. And she was loyal. You don't find that everyday."

"Look man.., you are not making me feel any better."

"My bad. Do you have a court date yet?"

"Mediation next week."

"Alright. So, you go in there. You looking good, smelling good and give her everything she wants. Just ask her for one thing, time. She'll give it to you."

"Man, I hope so."

"Aight, let's hoop..."

Lawrence and Jeff

"Well, I think that's everything, boss." Lawrence said as he closed his briefcase.

"Both clients should be happy, then." Jeff said as he glanced over some of the paperwork.

"I will admit. I was not looking forward to seeing you in court." Larry said as he laughed.

"The feeling is mutual, mate. You change from a regular bloke to a super hero in there."

"Well, we have to earn these rates to be able to justify charging them."

"True, indeed. Listen, did you want to grab a bite for lunch? There is a Thai restaurant around the corner." Jeff offered.

"I would, but I'm meeting Tina for lunch."

"Tina?"

"Oh, I'm sorry. Yeah. She's a client. I'm handling her divorce."

"Yeah. The name sounds familiar. Is that Kenna's friend?"

"It is. Did she tell you?"

"She did in fact. She didn't tell me you two were a thing. Kept that bit to herself."

"What makes you think that we are a thing?"

"Well, you used her name instead of saying "the client", didn't you? And your eyes lit up like your American holiday, July 4th, when you did."

Larry laughed at that.

"We do enjoy each other's company. I will say that."

"I'm glad. I am also sure that I don't have to remind you to be careful. She's married. To a millionaire, in fact. Who once waited three seasons to return a blatant foul on a player who had done it to him. The player was out for the rest of the season, mate. That bloak took his two game suspension with a smile. Who knows what he'll do if he finds out you two are together."

"I can't argue with you on that one. I saw that game. It was crazy. But I really like her. More than like, probably. So I'm not going to stop making her happy. And I'm committed to do that for as long as she makes me happy, and she does. If he wanted her, he wouldn't have had almost ten affairs. It's definitely his loss."

"Ten Affairs!!!! Is he mad?!!! Oh yeah. Have fun. She deserves it. Well done, you."

They both laughed at that.

"Well. I'm headed out then. I have had the taste for a Coconut Thai curry soup with shrimp ever since Kenna made it for me." He said as he stood up from his chair to head out.

I cleared my throat and pointed from him to the chair he had just been sitting in.

"...umm...have a seat Jeff. You don't get to lecture me and then drop a nugget like that on your way out the door."

He sat back in the seat with a smile.

"So, Kenna is cooking for her colleagues now? Because I've never even been offered a cracker in her office. Cold water and colder settlements, and a chai latte during a morning meeting. That is about the extent of it."

"She doesn't like crackers. More of a bangers and mash girl if I were to be completely honest..."

They both laughed out loud at this.

"..but seriously. She's been feeling down of late..."

"...And let me guess. You've been standing by with a pick me up. Hey, I am not mad at you. You've been crushing on her for as long as I can remember. It's about time you've made your move. Does she know how you feel about her?"

"I'm sure she does, yeah..."

"Uh oh. That doesn't sound good. Have you opened your British mouth and, in that accent that all the American girls love; an unfair advantage by the way; told her that you like her."

"It's a bit complicated it is.." Jeff started.

"Just the facts, counselor."

"No. We have been having a good bit of fun lately. A movie here, dinner and dancing there. I don't want to ruin it. Or our friendship besides."

"You need to tell her. Or you will, as sure as the sky is blue, be stuck in the friend zone. She'll start to invite you over to help her pick a sexy dress out for a date with someone else."

"Oh bite your tongue..." Jeff interjected.

"...then she'll tell you to close your eyes as she gets dressed in front of you for her date with him."

"You sound as if this is familiar territory for you, friend."

"Very much so. That's why I was sure to let Tina know, up front, that I was not looking for another friend."

"Indeed. Well, I hate to admit it. But, you are right, mate. I'll get right to work on it...."

"Or learn the different lipstick colors..." Lawrence added as Jeff again stood to leave. Earning him a middle finger and laugh from Jeff as he left.

Bobbi

I was so nervous. I had done art shows before. I had even been successful in selling my pieces. This was my first solo art show. I had worked so hard on making sure that every detail was perfect. I was happy for it, honestly. It took my mind from my abusive husband and the baby he had ripped from me.

He had been calling and emailing me since I was released from the hospital. I know my lack of communication was only serving to anger him more. The text and emails were proof of that. They went back and forth between missing and loving me and being sorry to what he was going to do to me if I did not come back to him.

I was nervous and confused. I had never ignored him and stayed away this long. I just couldn't look at him without thinking of my child. The child that I had carried within my body for months. I was just, sad. I tried to pretend in public, but, when I was alone in the condo my best friend gifted me, I drank wine, cried and created art in the spare bedroom she had converted into an art studio for me.

"This is amazing." A voice said, interrupting my thoughts.

I turned to see Dr. Lindsay standing behind me. My goodness what that lab coat was hiding should be illegal. He stood there in a pink fitted, short-sleeved button up with tan dress pants and loafers. I had to bring myself back and respond.

"Thank you, Dr. Lindsay. I didn't think you would make it tonight."

"Of course, I would. I told you I would. A promise is a promise. And, it's Kelvin.

"Right, Kelvin." I said with a smile.

"I ran into your friends outside. They told me you were still here. I would have come earlier, but I had can emergency to see to. I really am sorry.

"There's no need to apologize. I was one of your emergencies not too long ago. So, I completely understand. So, what do you think?"

"Your abstract work is beautiful, hauntingly so."

"Do you really think so?" I asked.

"Absolutely. Firstly, I'm impressed that you sculpt and paint. I mean, how?"

"I just create. I feel it first. Then it just takes shape. I never know which avenue that will take until I start working on the project. I try not to limit myself in what I'm doing. In what I'm feeling, ya know."

"Well, I can tell you one thing. It makes others feel."

"Thank you."

"No. Thank you for allowing me to see it. Well, I see it's pretty much cleared out in here. Am I holding you?"

"Oh, no. We're fine. The orders have been taken. The earlier crowd is usually huge..."

"Then it's just us stragglers." he said with a smile that started in his eyes.

"Exactly.."

From there, we walked around and spoke of music, and art. All of a sudden, he stopped in front of my work called "Broken". It was a woman looking into a mirror. Her face was flawless, but her reflection in the mirror was cracked into pieces.

"Magnificent...."

"Really? Thank you..."

"I want it. No. That is a gross understatement. I need it."

"Take it. It's my gift to you..."

With that, he turned and looked directly into my eyes. He then brushed a runaway strand of my hair from my face. Were we having a movie moment? I thought so. I'd never had one before. Not a love story anyway. I was quite sure of that. I mean, I could feel his energy, and it was good. Just then, we heard yelling.

"Bobbi, what the hell is this!?!?"

We both turned to see Jones walking quickly towards us.

"Oh, that's why you haven't been home. You out here whoring around with the doctor!!!"

I stood there, in shock and afraid. My body literally started to shake. I didn't know if I should run or curl up in a ball. He was wild-eyed and crazed. I had seen this look before. Too often, if I'm honest. It usually ended in me at the hospital.

When he was within arm's reach of me, clearly rearing up to grab me. Kelvin stepped in front of me and grabbed his arm before it could make contact, twisting it behind Jones's back.

"That's not how you treat women." He said. He then pushed Jones across the room.

Jones caught himself on one of my sculptures. He then turned around, even more upset now.

"This is between me and my wife. You need to leave us alone so we can talk." He said. His voice a shade lower and calmer now. "Bobbi, babe. Tell him we need to talk."

"I don't have anything to say to you. I've filed for divorce. Please leave. Just..go...please."

"Bobbi!!...get your ass over here...NOW!!!!!" His angry voice filled the space.

With that, he turned and kicked the sculpture over that had, only moments ago, saved him from falling on his face. I screamed out in shock and tried to make my way over to salvage what I could. I was stopped by Kelvin's arms.

"Not yet. Not until he leaves."

Just then, we heard police sirens. The art students where I taught were there to help me set up and take orders for experience and extra credit. They had heard and seen the commotion and called the police. They came in and asked us what was going on. About twenty minutes later, I was still in tears and Jones was in the back of the police car.

The whole time, Kelvin never left my side. After the police took our statements and left, taking Jones to cool off in a cell, Kelvin walked me to his car and helped me to sit on the passenger side. Once he was sure I was safe, he then went back and met with the students and spoke with them before coming back to the car.

They were worried for me and had offered to finish up the orders and to close up the gallery. He sat next to me and started the car up. He reached over and wiped my tears with his hands, gently.

"Are you ready to go?"

I nodded yes. I was more than ready.

"Where to?"

"Anywhere but here..."

"Say no more."

An hour later we were uptown at a jazz club with live music. I was so glad he chose to bring me here. I didn't feel much like dancing, but I swayed to the music in my chair with my eyes closed. Every time I opened my eyes, he was looking at me.

"Don't feel sorry for me." I said. "I brought this on myself. I know how he gets.."

"Absolutely not. Not one thing that you could do, or not do, would cause a real man to put his hands on you. Were you serious about filing for divorce?

"Yes...after the baby...I'm just ready to be rid of him..."

"I knew it. I knew he was to blame. Son of a bitch..."

"She is kind of a bitch..." I joked to lighten the mood. He got it and laughed with me.

Just then, a woman climbed the stage and started singing "Angel". It was one of my favorite songs and she was killing it. I was feeling a little better now. The wine helped, I'm sure. So I stood up and took his hand, leading him to the dancefloor. It was the perfect song. He had definitely been my Angel that night.

Later, we ended up back at the condo. We were sitting on the floor, in front of the fireplace, going through my vinyl record collection. He grabbed one of the records and turned to me wide-eyed like a child on Christmas.

"Am I looking at "Paradise" by the Temptations with Oh, mother on B-side...on vinyl? "

"Your eyes do not deceive you."

I took it from him and put it on. He started singing along. I could not believe how good he sounded. It reminded me of my daddy's voice before he died. That and his face were etched in my mind. He brought those memories, some of the only good memories of my childhood before everything fell apart.

"Boy, let me find out I have Mr. Kendricks right here with me this night." I said. He really did have a beautiful voice.

"I do a little something..." he said before he lifted me to my feet to dance while he sang to me.

"Why don't you cooommme to my island of paradise.." I began to sing.

He stepped back in shock. That wasn't the reaction I was expecting. All of a sudden, I was embarrassed.

"I'm sorry..."

"No, don't be. It's just that tonight was kind of heavy. I don't want to take advantage of you."

I smiled and walked back up to him and held his face in my hands.

"Well that's a shame. I guess i'll have to take advantage of you then." I responded as I unbuttoned his shirt.

"Are you sure?"

"More sure than I have been of anything in a long time."

With that he kissed me back. We made love right there on the rug in front of the fireplace. He then stood up, naked and looking like a Spartan from 300, and found a blanket so I wouldn't be cold. He brought water over from the fridge, which we both drank down.

"You're one of a kind. Like your pieces." He whispered into my ear.

I thanked him. With that he laid back, bringing me onto his chest and kissing my forehead. This was what I was missing. It was absolutely what I deserved. And I was going to enjoy it.

Caden/Tina/Lawrence

I walked into the conference room of my lawyer's office. There she sat. All smiles as her lawyer whispered something in her ear. My first thought was, wow, she looked soooo good. My next thought was, who is this clown sitting closely by my wife and making her light up like Paris at night?

I mean, they didn't even seem to notice us come in. There was something that made me uneasy down in my soul to see it. And I don't even talk like that. Oh yeah, I would be keeping my eyes on this crap. She was still my wife and I wanted her back. Even my lawyer looked a little surprised himself at what he saw. He interrupted their little, meeting...by clearing his throat.

"Hey, Todd. Caden, How are you?" Larry said as he stood to shake our hands.

"Tina..."

"Cade..."

He walked over to me, bent down until he was closer to me than he had been in a long time, and looked me eye to eye.

"Tina, Can we talk?" Cade asked before the lawyers even started the mediation.

"We're here to talk..."

"I mean alone. It's just that we haven't spoken in months."

"Cade, I think it's best to speak through your council." Larry chimed in.

"I think it's best you stay out of this...and it's Mr. Williams. We aren't friends."

"Cade, take a minute, please." His lawyer asked.

"Ok. But I just wanted to talk to my wife."

"Say what you need to say so we can get on with it." Tina said.

"Ok, so I'm willing to give you everything you want..."

"Wait a minute Cade. We haven't discussed this..." his lawyer said.

"..I just want one thing from you. Time..."

"Time? What does that mean exactly? Time to do what?" Tina asked

"Time to win you back..."

"Tuhhh...as if you could."

"Why are you so willing to throw everything away? Everything that we've built together and.."

She turned to look at her clown and asked. "Is he kidding?" She then asked the same of my lawyer before turning back to me. "You cheat on me, repeatedly and then accuse me of throwing everything away. You threw it away. YOU!!! She yelled, as the tears started to fall.

Her clown was too quick to comfort her. He put his arm around her, took his pocket square out and dabbed her eyes. *Oh HELL NO*. He was too comfortable. I didn't like this mess at all. I wanted to be the one comforting her and whispering in her ear. He had one arm on the table and the other around her chair. My lawyer and I looked at each other. Now I knew that I was not crazy. He saw this too. I shook it off so I could address my wife.

"Tee...just one more chance. Please bae."

"Mr. Williams, you say you will give my client everything she wants if she gives you time." The Clown spoke.

"That's correct..."

"And if she refuses?" he countered.

"Then I'll drag this divorce out as long as I can..."

"Now you're blackmailing me?" She asked incredulously.

"It may seem like that, but I'm really just fighting for us as hard as I know how. I broke it, you're right. Now let me heal it. With time."

"How much time?" she asked.

"Tina. You don't have to do this. He can drag it out, but you have a strong case." Her lawyer told her.

"Why are you so against me winning my wife back?" I asked him.

"I'm looking out for the best interest of my client..."

"Yeah man, so you say."

"Caden!!...how much time?" She yelled. She was obviously trying to distract me from whatever this was.

"Six months.." I said. Pressing my luck.

"Hell no.." she said, shaking her head vigorously.

"Three months..." was my next offer.

"And what if I don't want to reconcile after three months?" Tina wanted to know.

"Then I sign all the papers. You get everything you want. But you have to give it a try. A real chance. Meaning, if you're spending time with anyone else, that ends...today."

This time she looked at the clown the way she used to look at me. I didn't address it again. But I had my hands full. It would be a challenge, but I aimed to win. She agreed. Not because she wanted to, but because she wanted to be free. Here I was holding her freedom hostage. She would thank me in the end. When we were back together and living our best lives. She would see.

Tina and Larry

After Cade and his lawyer left, Larry stood, locked the door behind them and then lost it.

"What in the entire hell was that? Why did you agree to this time crap?"

"Calm down. You heard him. He'll make it painless and easy if I just pretend for three months."

"You did not have to agree."

"If you knew how bad I wanted to be free, you would know that I did."

"Free of who...him or me?" he asked out if nowhere.

"Where did that come from? We were speaking of my marriage."

"And now we're speaking of us."

"What do you want me to say? We haven't even named, *'us'*. And you know I'm just leaving a marriage of ten years. Not to mention being with him through college."

"Correction, you are now working on your marriage of ten years. For the next three months, right?"

I just sat there staring at him. I honestly didn't know where he was going with this. It would be clear in a few moments.

"I just want to know where we stand." He told me. Looking lost.

"I love spending time with you. You have been a great distraction from everything going on in my life right now. But it would be wrong of me to ask you to just stand by for three months."

"A distraction? Woman......" he said as he leaned back on the table.

I stood and went over to him. I took his head and touched my forehead to his. He was honestly hurting. I never wanted to hurt him. I thought I could learn to love him one day. But I didn't want to be selfish. I thought the best thing was to let him go until everything was worked out. He had other plans.

"How would it be fair to ask you to wait?" I tried to reason with him.

"I don't want fair. I want the woman that I've fallen in love with to tell me that it's me she wants. I want her to tell me to call her husband's lawyer and say, "See you in court." I want her to want me as much as she wants her freedom. Call me when you want the same things."

With that, he kissed me. Grabbed his satchel and left.

Jones

I had been sitting outside of the courthouse for three hours. I knew Kenna would be here. After calling her office and pretending to be a client with a hearing today. A temp gave me all of the information I needed. It had to be a temp.

I remembered that her secretary's name was Miracle. I had spoken with her on many occasions when planning my wife's thirtieth birthday party with her friends. Knowing they would probably try to whisk her away on some girl's trip, I acted first. Planning her a big birthday bash. Couldn't have her on some island getting her groove back with her girlfriends.

It was then, after being lost in thought, that I realized that Kenna had come out of the courthouse. She stopped to speak with the small group she was with. I guessed that they were her clients. I also imagined they had won. Their faces were all smiles. If I had lost, there wouldn't be a damn thing funny to me.

I stepped back behind a tree and waited to see her part from her party. A few minutes later, that's what happened. She came down the courthouse stairs and crossed the street. Stepping up on the curb right near the tree that semi-hide me. I stepped out quickly. Too quickly, I think. She let out a yell and then lifted her briefcase to strike a blow. I threw my hands up and called her nickname.

"Ken!!! Ken it's me, Jones!!"

For a moment I thought she still wanted to hit me. Though, eventually, she dropped it back down to her side.

"Jones. What in the hell! Are you completely gone?!? What do you want?"

"I'm sorry. I didn't mean to scare you. I just wanted to ask you a question."

"How did you know where I was? Have you been following me, weirdo?"

I may have taken offense to that. If it hadn't been the nickname she and Tina gave me in college. They decided I was when they caught me waiting and hiding in the dark across from a Que party that Bobbi had gone to with them until three in the morning.

"No. Of course not."

"Don't pretend it's not your Modis operandi..."

"No. I'm not in college any longer, Ken. Damn. And that was a long time ago."

"Then how did you know where I was? Answer quickly before I call a couple cop friends over." She said, looking across the street at three of them who were standing around talking.

"I called your office. Your temp told me."

"What the hell???" she called out.

"Don't blame them. I pretended to be a client."

"Your manipulation knows no bounds. What do you want?"

"Kenna, you know what I want. My wife. Can you..."

"Let me stop you right there. Don't even fix your lips to ask me to tell you where she is. You can get that out of your head right now."

"Ken. We've known each other a long time."

"Oh, I know. We all have. I am just sorry it took us so long to see you for who you are. Even longer for her to leave you. Thank God she is far away from you."

"That's rough, Kenna."

"Not nearly as rough as watching her in the hospital looking at an ultrasound of her dead baby." She said with bubbling anger in her voice.

I leaned against the tree. I had no argument. I knew that Kenna nor Tina would ever give up their friend's location. But I was desperate and willing to try anything. I was trying to think and she started to walk away.

"No. Wait, wait. Can you at least give her a message?"

"Sure Jones. What would you like for me to tell her?"

I heard the sarcasm in her voice. This message may well not reach her at all. But I had to try.

"Please, tell her that I'm so so so sorry. That I love her and I'm going to change. My brother is helping me to get into anger management. Please, just come home." I begged.

"Uh huh. Anything else?" She asked, obviously not moved in the least.

"No. that's it."

"Fine. I have to go. Don't follow me again. Oh, and take a shower, Jones. You are a mess."

With that, she left me there. Standing near the tree and no closer to my wife.

Jeff and Larry

"Linda, Can you come in here." I asked my secretary over intercom.

"Sure thing, Jeff."

She came in my office with her tablet where she took down everything that I needed and made a list. She was super- efficient.

"Call Mr. Todd and tell him we have a settlement offer and schedule him for this week to come in and discuss it. Also, have Vicki, the new paralegal, look into the Fowler case for me. I may need John, our investigator on it, so shoot him an email as well, yeah? This bloak is a slippery one but I know he's hidden some funds somewhere. Lastly, send a bouquet of daisies and lilacs over to McKenna Dade. Oh, and add a bit of chocolate with it."

She smiled as she took that down.

"Should I send any message with the flowers and chocolate?"

"Umm..sure. Address it "To a worthy adversary who knows when to settle."

"That's right. You two have just finished the Spencer case."

"We did at that. She was absolutely brilliant. Got her client a great deal. He'll be chuffed to bits with it. That will be all, darling. Thanks."

As she was headed out, I looked up and saw Larry. He saw me through the door as well and I waved him in.

"Come on in, mate. Have a seat. Did we have an appointment then?" I said, trying to pull my calendar up.

"No. I just needed to talk, man."

"Well ok. What's on your mind then?"

"Tina.."

"Kenna's friend. Yeah. How's is going?"

"It's not."

"That's a shock. When I last saw you it was all heart eyes. What happened?"

"We had mediation with her husband. He threw the proverbial wrench, as it were, in my plans. Her husband offered her an uncontested divorce..."

"Well that sounds..." I started.

"....if she promised to try to make it work for three months...if not he'd tie her up in court for years."

".......Like complete and utter rubbish. What did she say of it?"

"She wants her freedom."

"So, she agreed...and what of you?"

"Right?!?!...that's what I said."

"So, you asked her to choose?"

"I guess you can say that."

"Between you and him?"

"No. Between me and her freedom from him."

"And you're here looking like you haven't slept a wink in days. So I'm thinking she chose her freedom.."

"I haven't, not in three weeks. And I haven't heard from her in as long. So, I'm guessing so."

"Ouch...that's a kick in the nads."

"Swift and hard."

"Do you know how they're getting on?"

"No. I haven't spoken with her. And I don't think I want to know. Did you know that she has only been with two men. Myself and her husband."

"No kidding. You don't find that anymore, I'll tell you that."

"I miss her. So, I came here so you could tell me to get over it."

"Right. It seems like I could tell you that. But would it work?"

"Probably not."

"And, is it what you want? To get over it?"

"Absolutely not..."

"Then I should save my words for someone who will listen then, yeah?"

"Probably."

We both laughed at that.

"I will tell you this. I'm sure she cares for you. But she's wanted her freedom for longer than she's wanted you. Knowing that, you can't ask her to take a chance with that then. And once she has it, you can be with her. Hey, it looks like there's some sunshine for you."

"See. I knew I came here for a reason. Thanks bro."

"No problem..."

He stood to go.

"Now I have to get over to court. By the way. Have you made it out of the friend zone yet?"

"I'm clawing my way out as we speak."

We laughed again and he left me there to think. He was right. It was time for me to make my move. Enough subtle gestures. I needed to tell her how I felt. I hit the intercom.

"Linda. Have you placed that order for delivery yet?"

"I was just going to.."

"Forget it. I'm going to take it myself."

"Well good for you." She said.

That remained to be seen.

Kelvin and Bobbi

I walked up behind her in her art studio. She sat there on a chair, wearing one of my tee shirts I had left at her condo, sketching. Miguel's "Adorn" had just gone off and his new song, "Coffee", followed in rotation. I loved that she was an old soul with a modern twist. I wrapped my arms around her and started to sing in her ear...

"I wish I could paint our love. These moments in vibrant hue.."

"Mmmm....I beat you to it..." she said.

With that, she flipped her sketch book pages and I saw exactly what she meant. She had sketched the most passionate sunrise. It was pink, purple, blue and soft. It overlooked a mountaintop. On the mountaintop lie a woman with her hand outstretched, as if trying to touch it. Her eyes closed, as if dreaming. The other hand clasp over her heart.

"Do you see it?" she asked with her soft voice barely above a whisper.

"I do..."

"It's how you make me feel." She whispered. Like I can touch it.

"It's not fair..." I said..

"What?" She asked...

"That you can show me how I make you feel, but there are no words that can express my feelings for you...and I can't draw..."

"There are other ways." she said.

With that, I came and stood in front of her. I took the sketch book from her hand and set it on the table. I picked her up out of the chair and carried her to the ledge of the picturesque window and made love to her. I didn't want to rush it. I wanted her to feel exactly what she meant to me.

She wanted me to feel the same as she rolled over and climbed on top of me. My goodness, where had she been my thirty-eight years? How could anyone want to do anything other than water her, nurture her and watch her grow? To do anything else would be robbing yourself as well as her.

We both finished together. She then lay on my chest.

"Did I make you late for your rounds? Those babies aren't going to deliver themselves." She joked.

"You have court today, so I cleared my schedule. And they pretty much do deliver themselves." I teased her back.

You're going with me?" She said as she sat up to look in my eyes. It was a look of appreciation mixed with disbelief.

"Yes, I am. Where else would I be other than next to you. I just want you to know that it takes heart to do this. I am so proud of you.

She kissed me and laid back down. I knew she was nervous. But she had me.

"I could use some coffee..." she said.

"According to Miguel, we just had our fill."

We both laughed at that.

"I'll go put some on anyway. Are you hungry?" She asked as she stood to head to the kitchen.

I grabbed her by the hand and pulled her back to me...

"Starved..." I said as I stared into her eyes. Man, those eyes. They weren't fair. We started swaying back and forth to the song still playing in my head. I picked her up as a groom would his bride and carried her to the bedroom. She laughed the whole way as I started singing to her again though the song was long ago over.

"......When we face the sun, you'll know for sure that I'm all yours...I'm all yours now baby...."
I now knew what my job was. It was more than caring for patients and delivering babies. My job was to protect her and make her laugh for the rest of her life.

A few hours later, we arrived at the courthouse. We were met by Bobbi and Tina. I loved that she had friends that cared for, protected and loved her so much. She didn't have any family worth mentioning so their bond was all the more special.

We sat in the waiting area chit chatting. We were there about twenty minutes before her husband came in. He looked sad and unkempt. He was definitely presenting as a man who was losing control. This worried me. Abusers were known to become more dangerous when losing it. Their victims were in the most danger then as well. It worried me because I couldn't always be with her. I had a practice to run.

He looked over at each one of us with rage. I could tell he wanted to say something to her, but the temporary restraining order prohibited that. We were there to petition the court to have it extended. After another few minutes in the waiting area, they called their case. We all went in with her. She and her lawyer sat at the table across from him and his lawyer. We sat in the row right behind her.

The judge asked her lawyer to provide any reasons that he should extend the restraining order. This was required since Jones tried to argue that the order was not needed. He tried to persuade the court that he just had a one-time loss of his temper. I think he was expecting her to agree with what he said and back down.

This had always been the case before. Her loyalty to and simultaneous fear of him had protected him from ever being held responsible for his actions. He was still looking to cash in on those feelings. We knew that he was still banking on her coming back to him. He would find out how much his grasp had been loosened when her lawyer started to answer the judge's question.

The truth is, not even I was not prepared what her lawyer presented. It was clear he wasn't either. He was used to her covering for him. Not anymore. The blankets were definitely off and he was not handling the cold well. He hung his head and clenched his fists at his side when the evidence was presented.

Her lawyer had hospital records going back at least five years. She had endured more than even I knew. He started to naming injuries starting with a *broken nose, collarbone and scapula.* She had also endured *bruised limbs and organs* from being brutally kicked. This fool had even gone so far as to hold her hostage in their home when she threatened to leave.

I could see her wiping her eyes as the words were read. She was rocking back and forth and shaking as if she was reliving each attack. I reached across and took her hand. This really angered him. I could see his heavy breathing deepen and teeth clenched to match his fist.

The judge had heard enough. Stopping her lawyer, he turned to Jones and unleashed on him.

"You, sir, are a coward."

"Your honor.." his lawyer tried to object in his thick, *My Cousin Vinny* accent. All he lacked was the leather jacket.

"No, Sal. I can address your client. Mr. Lindsay, Only a coward would put his hands on a woman. To cause such damage is unthinkable. I wish she were my daughter. Heck, my niece, sister or next door neighbor even. I'd have given you the what for after the first time. But I am not. I wish I could throw you in jail right now, but I cannot."

The judge then turned to Bobbi.

"Young lady, I cannot imagine how afraid you must be of him. To have endured this brutality, and the loss of a child due to his actions is unconscionable. For all of these reasons, and for your safety, I am granting your request. Nothing good will come of you being anywhere near him. I am so sorry for your loss and all the pain you have endured. Now, I don't know where your father is, but allow an old man and father of three girls to give you some advice. Don't ever go back. And you would be wise to press charges on him for at least the most recent attack. Then I can put him where he belongs, in jail. When do you go to court for the divorce proceedings?"

"Next month." her lawyer responded.

"Very well. I'm glad to hear it."

He extended the order and encouraged her, again, to press charges. After that, we were all dismissed from the courtroom. He burst out the courtroom doors and almost ran from the courthouse. His lawyer trying to catch up with him. We gave him a few minutes to get to his car and leave.

I could tell that she was beyond nervous. The tears were coming and she was still shaking. We tried to comfort her. Kenna had to be in court herself and Tina had a meeting. I assured them that she was safe with me. Other than that, they would not have left her side. They hugged her, gave her some words of encouragement and then left.

We found a quiet corner and I walked her through some breathing exercises. Once she had calmed down, she and I walked slowly and quietly from the courthouse, hand in hand.

"What are you thinking?" She asked me.

"That I had no idea...I mean, you told me he had hit you but I just was not prepared for what I heard."

"It's not something that I like to talk about."

"...not in words anyway." I said.

"What do you mean?"

"Your art tells the story."

"You aren't wrong in that assessment, doctor. You have no idea how many paintings and sculptures have been created to the sounds of my tears. And viewed through black eyes.."

I stopped and hugged her again. I just wanted to wrap her in my arms and let her know she was safe now. She deserved no less than that.

"No more black eyes. No more broken bones. You should only ever cry tears of joy."

She nodded her head as the tears rolled again..

"Hey. What did we just say?"

"No. these are happy tears, I promise." she assured me. Taking my hand.

"Oh...well then that's allowed..." I said and we both smiled and headed to my car.

"Where to?" I asked her like I always did.

"I need food. For some reason, I am starving..." she said with a smile through her tears.

"...I wonder why..." I said as we pulled off.

Jones

My lawyer caught up to me and called my name. I finally stopped, right outside of the building and turned to face him and hear what he had to say.

"Jones, geez. Make me chase ya why don't cha." He said, out of breath.

"What Sal? What do you have to say after allowing the judge to tear me a new one?"

"He's the judge. They are allowed to have their say before they pass judgement. Other lawyers wouldn't have even tried to get him to change course at all."

"Fine."

"Do you understand what just happened in there?" Sal asked me.

"I'm not an idiot. I understand. I can't see my own wife."

"That is an understatement. You cannot contact her, her friends or anyone in her life. No calls. No visits to her work. No ambushing her friends. No letters written on paper airplanes and flown into her window. Nothing."

"Again. Not an idiot."

"I just want to make sure that you understand that you could go to jail if you violate the order."

"Jail? For speaking to my wife? Perfect." I said seething in anger.

"She doesn't want to see you, Jones. You have to understand that. And I've worked with your father and family for years. So, I think I can be honest. She has damn good reason to be afraid of you. If even half of what I know is true. However, I am your lawyer and only vested in your well-being. Now, I'm going to tell you this. That judge in there would love nothing more than to see on his desk a violation of his order, by you. He would give you the maximum. Of that I have no doubt."

"Which is?"

"The fact that you want to know how long you could be in jail worries me."

"How long Sal??"

"One year and, not that money is an issue to you, a five thousand dollar fine."

"One year. Okay. And what about the doctor?"

"Who?"

"The guy she had in there with her. That was her doctor. This is the second time I've seen him with her. Can we get him to stay away from her?"

"No. On what grounds, Jones?"

"I don't know. You're the lawyer. You tell me. I don't want another man moving in on my property."

"Your property? For goodness sake, Jones. She's a human being. And, in case Jack and Nessa never told you, take a lesson from me. Firstly, actions have consequences. And lastly, you can't have everything you want. You just can't." He told me in obvious exasperation.

I didn't care what he said. I was heartbroken and I just want to see my parents. I needed to get away from this whole ordeal.

"Thank you, Sal. I heard you. But I have to go and clear my head."

"Yes. Good idea. Clear and level heads prevail. I'll check in with you soon."

I nodded my understanding and hastily left the courthouse. Headed right to my mom's. She would know what to do.

Caden and Tina

"You look great, Tutu." I told her as I pulled her chair out.

"Thank you, Caden." She replied dryly.

"I ordered you a glass of wine." I told her.

"Thank you..." she offered in the same tone.

"I remembered how much you like this restaurant. We used to have so much fun here. It doesn't look like it's changed that much."

"Hmm.."

This was going to be harder than I thought. I didn't know what to say to her to break the ice. So, I reminded her of her promise.

Tee, you said you would try."

"I'm here. Am I not?" She said as she looked around the restaurant.

"Showing up is not trying. Especially since you looking this good has always been effortless."

I saw her try to hide a smile.

"Just what are you expecting? That I will come in here and laugh and joke and reminiscence with you? Okay, let's do that, reminisce. So, one evening, after making love to my husband. That would be you. I grabbed my laptop to do some work with my sister. As I was sitting online, sipping wine, and chatting with my sister, all of a sudden, a message came through."

"Tutu..."

"No. let's go back down memory lane, as the late great Minnie Riperton said. Who was it? You may ask. Well, this particular time, because there have been many." She said as she leaned in for effect. "It was Breeana. She was so nice. But you already know that, I'm sure. Right?"

"Don't do this." I pleaded with her, looking around to make sure no one was listening in.

"Why not? I mean we could have talked about it in counseling, but you opted out of that." She said as she continued to drink from her wine glass.

"And I'm sorry. But I'm going now. I am trying to work on me so that I can be better for you."

She sat back in her chair and did the slow, sarcastic clapping that you never want to be on the receiving end of. It is never good.

"Well goody goody for you."

Now, can we get back to Me. Breanna?"

I realized I was not getting out of this. To be honest, I didn't deserve to. My therapist said I needed to allow her to express her pain, no matter how uncomfortable it made me. Some I nodded her on.

"Thank you. So, she asked me how I was doing and if I was Cade's wife. As soon as I said yes, she sent me the picture. Do you remember the picture?"

"Yes. I remember."

"The picture of my husband in her bed. Her with her tacky feathers and mismatch sheets. I mean, did you at least buy her a comforter set? Well...I guess not. If you had, maybe she wouldn't have been messaging me. You have to make better investments." she said as she downed the rest of the wine and waved the sommelier over for another.

"Tina...I'm.."

"....sorry...right you always are. Do you know how many times you've broken my heart?"

"Yes, I do." I said in a hushed tone. My heart sank just watching the hurt in her eyes.

"Really. Do tell." She said as she cocked her head to the side awaiting my answer.

"Seven..." I answered.

"Tahahahahahaa!!!! Oh please. I asked how many times you broke my heart. Not how many mistresses I know about. You couldn't possibly know because I have lost count myself. Now you want me to sit here and try. The only reason you're trying now is because I stopped trying with YOU!" She screamed.

"You're right about all of it. I messed up. I should have done right by you. But please give me the chance now..please.." I pleaded.

"Do what you want?" she said as she ordered another glass.

"You should eat something." I told her as I buttered a piece of the warm pumpernickel bread she loved and handed it to her. She took it and bit into it.

"Even though I know I have no right, Can I ask you something?" I asked.

"I guess..." she said, buttering another piece of bread.

"Have you been seeing someone?"

She put the bread on the plate and sat back in her chair and studied my face..

"Why do you ask that?"

"Because, I'm no fool. I saw how you and your lawyer looked at each other, the jerk."

"Next question..." she said...

That was all I needed. When Tina said that, it meant I was right. I had known her long enough to know this.

"Ok. Do you love him?"

"I love me. And I love being happy and that's all I have for you on the topic."

"Fair enough." is what my mouth said. That certainly is not what my heart said.

I tried to keep from her the pain I was feeling to think of someone else being with her. I was her first. I should have been her last. Instead I had broken her heart, repeatedly. Now here I was clumsily trying to piece it back together. I know I should have thought of someone else loving her before. But I never thought she would leave.

I don't know why I didn't think it. She was a smart cookie. My lawyer had found that all of a sudden, she AND her family were basically real estate moguls. She obviously listened to her mother. I know she didn't need half, but she had earned it. She had put up with my crap since I saw her in Sociology class on the that day. She was beautiful and focused. She had gotten me through that and much more.

As I watched her eat bread and look at everything but me, It came to me. I needed to meet her where she was. She wasn't ready to talk to me, but I knew who she would talk to. That was her two best friends. I would arrange a trip for them to a place she always wanted to go but I had never had the chance to take her. England.

The Girls Take England

"Cade is pulling out all the stops, is he not?" Bobbi asked as we sat in the the back of the car he had reserved to be at our beck and call.

"Yes he is. I will give him that." I agreed.

"I feel like I'm being bought." Kenna added.

"Well, my dear, that's because you are. And I would know what that looked like." I again answered.

We all laughed at that.

"I started to refuse the trip, but I've wanted to come here forever. He always had somewhere else to be. Now I get to experience this, but with my girls."

"Awww...should we not be yelling out the window or sunroof or something?" Bobbi asked.

"As if you ever would...." Kenna teased.

"You don't think I will?"

"I know you won't.."

Kenna had barely gotten the words out of her mouth before Bobbi was hanging out the window screaming..

"Hello England!!!!!!!"

"Oh, my goodness. Get that girl in here!!!" I said, causing more laughter.

As soon as we pulled up to the Mandarin Oriental Hyde Park, London, Kenna said..

"Well, he's winning me back over.."

"Geez, you're so easy girl. A five star hotel is all it takes?" I asked.

"Yes. Add Margaritas. If he arranged for a mixologist to follow us around, I'LL marry him."

We all laughed again. It was the best medicine. We checked in and got some sleep. The time change was rough. We woke up and headed for the spa. It was beautiful. Tnd we could all use some pampering. We changed into robes made from clouds, I'm sure. They were so soft, with slippers to match.

We sat getting manicures and pedicures and just having girl talk. We headed to our massages next. I chose a hot stone massage. Bobby explained to them that she had some injuries and sometimes still had pain. They offered her a Sports massage by someone certified in it. And Kenna went with a Swedish.

That's where it got real. We let our feelings pour out.

"So, Bobbi. How's everything with the divorce?" Kenna asked.

"It's going, he just refuses to sign the papers. He's putting up a fight on everythng.

"He suuuucks..." Kenna dragged out.

"Facts....but you know what's really odd?"

"What?" I asked.

"He really has stopped contacting me. When I first got the order, he didn't care. Now he's kind of fallen in line."

"Isn't that what we want?" I inquired of her.

"Yes, but knowing him, he's had too much time to plan revenge. Or, maybe I'm just being paranoid."

"Absolutely not. You have every reason to be nervous." Kenna assured her.

"Well, at least you have a bodyguard." I said.

We all erupted into laughter again. The three of us knew one thing. How to laugh. Even when things we tough.

"Speaking of the doctor. How well is he guarding your body?" Kenna asked.

"Head of Security status, girl. Head to toe."

"Speaking of bodyguards, when are you planning to let that sexy young lawyer close the deal?" I asked.

We're just friends." Kenna answered.

"Lies and propaganda. I've seen him in a tailored suit, no one is just friends with that." Bobbi added.

"Girlll, If that isn't the 8th deadly sin. Then his accent to boot." I added.

"I know. I'm not blind or deaf. And he's been bringing me gifts and we've been hanging out. But I don't want to date someone I work with. " I told you this before.

"Someone help her. Alright, first of all, you do not work with him. You two have gone against each on cases but he is at a different firm. So, let's stick to the facts please, counselor." I reminded her.

"True." she conceded pretty easily.

"So now what's the excuse?" I wanted to know.

"I'm scared. Ok. Stop brow beating me!" she declared.

"Scared of what?" Bobbi asked.

When she did not reply, I knew what it was she wasn't saying to us.

"She's afraid she will end up like us." I answered for her.

"Is that true?" Bobbi asked. "It's okay if it is." Bobbi assured her.

"Well, yes. Look at you two. Beautiful, intelligent and talented. If your marriages don't work, how the hell will mine?" she inquired.

"Oh honey, it's okay to be afraid. Yours will work because you know what you want. We were children when we got into these marriages. We didn't even know ourselves. And we grew apart."

"And it didn't help that Jones beat the tar out of me. And Cade couldn't keep it in his pants." Bobbi added.

"She's not wrong you know." I said with a laugh. "Don't let our marriages scare you. You go into it when you're ready. Know yourself, know him and make the right decision for you. And you know we have your back no matter what." I promised her,

"Awwww" she said. As she drew a heart in the air with her finger.

"Sooo extra." Bobbi said.

"So, to totally change the subject, what's going on with you and Larry?"

"I have no clue. I really care for him. It's just that I'm trying to break free from Cade after over ten years of marriage. I just don't know if I should get into another serious relationship. Which is what he wants and deserves. Or if I should take time to myself and enjoy my freedom. But Larry is everything I wish Cade was. I don't know. Goodness I need a drink. "

"Quite the dilemma." Bobbi said.

"Really, that's it? I need advice and all you can tell me is what I already know. Next."

"Yeah. You have to make this choice on your own. Are you leaving Cade because you want freedom? Or are you leaving Cade because you want better." Bobbi added.

"Thank you. That's what I needed, some philosophical stuff. I guess I don't really want freedom as much as I want freedom from Cade and all the hurt and pain he's caused me. I was ready to be a wife until death did us part. I just couldn't handle everything Cade had done. I think I've made my decision and without a glass of wine."

We all laughed and then settled down to enjoy the rest of our massages. The rest of our trip was just great. We visited some pubs Jeff had suggested and visited Big Ben as well. He also made arrangements for us to eat at restaurants with chefs such as Phil Howard.

The most important thing, I think, is that we made some real progress on what we wanted. Life for all of us would change when we got back to the states. We had no idea how much. But until then, we would have fun here.

Bobbi

The girls were still asleep when I left the hotel. We had a suite each with our own bedroom and bathroom. So, I had gotten up, showered and dressed and grabbed my sketch pad. I left them a note so that they wouldn't worry. I also left them the car and caught a cab. I was in another country. One that had actual castles. I couldn't wait to see Buckingham palace, Hampton Palace and the tower.

I also needed to clear my head. My art always helped me get it out. It had been jumbled of late. I had not been sleeping really. I was actually glad for the time change. But even with that, I only napped for maybe two hours.

I worried about Kelvin and I and wondered if we were safe. I also wondered if I should be hopping into anything right now. My feelings could change from one day to the next. They would go from anger, to fear to sadness to incredible loss and guilt. I had too much baggage.

I would think about the baby I had lost and just cry. Other times, I would just sit and relive some of the abuse. I would think about the time he dragged me through the house by my hair. I still had hair thinning in the back because of that.

These thoughts could come crashing in at any time. They would cause me to feel as if a weight was on my chest. As if I couldn't breathe. I was so stupid. How could I have been so stupid? I found myself standing in front of Buckingham palace, bawling. People walked back and forth, some noticed and others didn't.

I wiped my face and pulled my sketch pad out of my over-sized hobo bag. As soon as the pencil hit the paper, my chest began to feel lighter. The guards standing at the gate were something to see. I had wished and prayed ever since I was a child for someone to protect and care for me. For the longest time I thought that was Jones.

Now that I could actually see and had someone who seems to genuinely care for me, was I even deserving of him? I was confused. The bigger the piece I was working on, the less I felt. By the time I started in on the windows, I was numb. Which, if I remember Psychology 202 correctly, is not a good sign either. But for right now, it beat crying myself to sleep.

Kenna

I giggled as I read the text message. Jeff and I had been in constant contact since I had left for England. He was like our own digital tour guide. He had provided us with places to go eat and tourist spots. This time he wanted to know what our plans were for the day. Before I could answer, his text had become a phone call.

"Hello."

"Well then, you're over there enjoying our posh London accommodations as the rest of us toil away."

"Toil? Oh please. You have probably agreed to three, million dollar settlements before you had your tea and Jammie Dodgers."

"Oh, good girl. You are learning our English ways. Bravo. And, though I like a good biscuit, those Jammie dodgers do have their place then, don't they?"

I laughed before answering, "They do, but I think we were almost run out of Yorkshire for me putting two sugars and no milk in my tea..."

"Tourist, tsk tsk. And in Yorkshire no less. It surprises me you weren't run out by proper Yorkshire lasses. If you think Philly and New York women are tough. Spend time with one of them."

"I think I met one. The look she gave me when watching me make my tea was less than welcoming." I laughed.

"I see I will have to take you back myself and give you a proper introduction to British life then, won't I?" he said. Except I was pretty sure he was serious.

"That would be lovely." I said in my best British accent.

"Well done, you." He said as I heard him clapping in the background.

We then laughed at how horrible it truly was.

"Well, to your question of our plans, we were heading out to Edinburgh. There is the castle, that we all want to see, of course. Then there is an art festival we think may cheer Bobbi up."

"I am sure it is. But leave your night free, I've a surprise for you."

"A surprise?"

"Sure...should I tell you now or leave it until tonight?"

"Jeffrey, if you don't tell me right now.."

"Ok, ok darling." he laughed. " I've left concert tickets at the Royal Naval college for tonight."

"A concert? Really? Who???" I asked like an excited child.

"You guys will be seeing are Adele, Duffy, Ems, Sam, Ed, Zayn Malik and Tim."

"Oh, my goodness, I love Adele and Duffy, and one direction was my guilty grown black woman pleasure. But don't laugh when I ask this, promise?"

"No promises, but please ask."

"I'm pretty sure Sam is Sam Smith and Ed is Mr. Sheeran, Who are Ems and Tim?"

"Oh, right. Sorry then. Emeli Sande and Labrinth. You have heard of them, yeah?"

I jumped up out of the bed and started running in place and pumping my fist like an excited schoolgirl. I didn't want him to know I was such a geek, so I regained my composure before I answered him.

"Of course. I love them. I guess I'm not posh enough to know them by their nicknames. Unlike you I see. Did you go to school with them or something?"

He paused for maybe two seconds before he answered.

"Or something. Now, do you think your friends will be up to it?"

"Hells yeah!! Thank you sooo much, Jeff.

"No worries, darling."

"Can I ask you a question?"

"Anything..."

"Why are you so nice to me?"

"I thought that was obvious. I want you to be happy." He replied.

"Well, mission accomplished. Thank you so much."

"Of course. Now you lot go, get on with your day then. It's going to be a long one."

We ended our call and I went screaming through the suite. Bobbi and Tina thought I was having a mental break. Once I had told them what it was that had me so excited, they joined in. We must have looked absolutely ridiculous dancing around singing "Next to Me."

We had more surprises. The seats were so close, you would think that we were part of the show. During an intermission, just after Emeli Sande's set had ended, one of her people found us.

"Pardon me, are you the ladies Kenna, Bobbi and Tina."

"We are..." I asked with question in my voice.

"Ms. Sande would like to meet you in her dressing rooms."

We all looked at each other. When he turned and we started to follow, Bobbi grabbed my hand and whispered in my ear...

"WTF"

"I know right..."

We were introduced to her and she was everything.

"You ladies are stunning. Well, don't just stand there, come in, sit."

We did as were instructed.

"Alright then. Which of you obvious American models is McKenna?"

"Kenna, please." I answered.

"Right, nice to meet you. Jeff has mentioned you. When he called asking for tickets, I was happy to do it."

Just then Tim, better known as Labrinth, knocked and entered. Tina was used to being around stars and celebrities. Bobbi and I were not as accustomed to it. Our mouths dropped when that little handsome piece of chocolate stuck his head in the door.

"My ladies." He greeted us. Ems, are these LM's friends then?"

"They are.."

"Lovely."

Bobbi mouthed "LM?"

I shrugged my shoulders. Probably a nickname, I thought. We talked about our stay there and a little about ourselves.

"I must ask, when is LM coming back home for a visit? We have missed him terribly." Emelie asked."

"I have no idea."

"Right then. He and his mates owe me and mine a proper football match. He ran across the pond to hide, hasn't he then?" Tim said as we all laughed.

We left having met every entertainer on the bill. We had pictures and their autographs too. I definitely owed him a movie and a friendly dinner.

Tina

My phone kept ringing. I thought whoever it was would eventually get the picture and just hang the heck up. No, they didn't. The girls and I had gotten in late, or technically early from the concert and I was sleeping in. I finally rolled over and grabbed the phone. It was my sister. I said a quick prayer everything was ok.

"Hello.."

"Hey sis. You sleep?"

"I was.."

"In the middle of the day? What are you sick or something?"

"No. I'm not sick. I'm in the UK, so it is not the middle of the day here."

"The UK? What in the world are you doing there?"

"I'm on a girl's trip."

"A girl's trip is to the Bahamas, Cancun or Barbados. Not England. What are you really doing there?"

"Girl, what are you being an irkbox for? A girls' trip be can to anywhere."

"Because I can irk you. You did it to me your whole life. Anyway, I called because mommy told me that you left Cade. I wanted to see what was going on and check in on you."

"I'm ok.."

"You left your husband, you are not ok. What's up for real."

I started bawling. Just like that. I was even shocked myself. I thought I had cried my last tears over him. Sometimes all it takes is that one aunt, cousin or sister-friend to say *"Girl cut the crap and be real."*

"Aww TT....what's wrong? Talk to me."

"He just couldn't stop cheating on me. Like, what was it about me that made him have to look somewhere else? Was I not pretty enough? Small enough. Maybe these girls know tricks in the bed that I'll never learn..."

"Oh no you dont. This don't have nothing to do with you. You know he just out there being a man. Men mess up. Especially men like him. He's a tall, good looking athlete and worth millions. He may as well have a target on his back for these homewreckers."

"I know. But they aren't married to me. He is."

"Well, what is he saying?"

"He wants to work it out."

"You know that he does. He knows what he has."

"We went to mediation and he asked for three months to convince me to stay married. If I do it, he'll give me whatever I'm asking for in the divorce."

"I think that's a great deal girl. What do you have to lose?"

"The rest of my dignity. My mind. Quite possibly my freedom."

"Your freedom?" she asked, sounding confused.

"Yes. Because if I do decide to give him another chance, and he does it again, I may just have to kill him."

She started laughing and I joined in through my tears. After joking about ways to kill him and deciding on going full out Gerard Butler in the movie, "Law-Abiding Citizen", she got real with me.

"Listen. I'm not speaking from anywhere but love and experience."

"Experience?"

"Yes. It wasn't something I made a news broadcast about, but my husband had an on-going affair that lasted three years."

I sat straight up in bed. How had this slipped passed me. Well, you know what, even though my family was close, we all had our secrets. I listened when she laid it all out. There was even a child in question. The girl came clean and admitted it was her husband's baby. Yes, apparently, she was married as well. After my brother in law had paid her child support AND hush money.

Hell, after hearing their story I had forgotten about Cade and I for a moment. I finally asked her how they fixed it.

"Prayer, therapy and hard work. We're still working on it. It takes time, but he's your husband, so you do it..."

"Well. I've made it more complicated."

"Girl, you always do. How?"

"After I separated from him, I started seeing someone else."

"Goodness, girl. A Maury episode in the making. Ok, tell him you're working on your marriage and let that man get on with his business."

"Well, see what had happened was, he's my lawyer."

"Oh, oh. I just can't even deal with you!!!!."

"I didn't mean for it to happen. We got to know each other and one thing led to the other."

"Well, at least tell me it was good."

"I can't tell you that...Because it was more than good girl..."

"It always is when you creeping. You know that you have to tell Cade, right?"

"He knows. He figured it out when he saw us together at mediation."

"And what did he say?" she inquired next. In true sister form.

"That was the other stipulation. I had to stop any relationships I may have been in. And, I haven't seen Larry since. He was pissed. He said he wants me. It's just a mess. Then Cade sent us here.."

"Now I see. It's a get my wife back trip where he sent your friends with you to win them over to his side. I told you it wasn't a girl's trip." She laughed.

"Ha Ha..."

All of a sudden I heard crying. My niece was woke.

"Aww...what's wrong with munchkins??" I said in my aunty voice.

"Come get her and ask her."

"You know I do and will. She has her own room at my house and you know it."

"I know. Well, she'll be packed and waiting. She just woke up so let me go. But think about what I said. He's your husband, not your boyfriend or a fling. If it doesn't work, at least you can say you tried everything and your conscience is clear....ok...she just went up an octave. Kisses..."

"Kisses..."

After we hung up, I laid back in the bed and thought, for a long time. Maybe it wasn't over with Cade just yet.

Larry and Cade

I stepped out of my car and saw Cade sitting on the trunk of his sports car. What did he want, was all I could think. Though, I can't say I didn't expect to have a conversation with him at some point. I walked over to him.

"Mr. Williams, you really shouldn't be here without your lawyer."

"I'm here to talk to you about my wife."

"With me?"

"Don't play dumb. I know you are seeing her."

"What exactly can I do for you, Mr. Williams?"

"You can step off and let me fix my marriage. She acts like she doesn't want to do it. I know it's because of you."

"Well, first of all, you are the one who broke it. So why should she have to fix it? Also, I haven't seen her since our meeting. Now, if you aren't making progress, well, that's just the repercussions of your own adulterous actions."

"No, it's because you did something to her..."

I laughed out loud at that. I had done more to her than he knew.

"Is something funny?"

"Yeah, you. You are hilarious and a little sad. You want to know what I did to her? Get a pen so you can write this down. I treated her like the queen that she is, that's q-u-e..."

"Don't be smart, dog...." he said as he hopped off the car. He was 6'6. But I was no slouch at 6'3 and we both were in shape. So, if he meant to intimidate me, he was mistaken. I didn't back down. The Philly in me didn't allow it.

"You didn't value her then and you don't now and she's fed up with your lies..."

"Don't tell me how my wife feels dog. You don't know her."

"Yeah, you keep telling yourself that. I think out of the two of us, you're the one who doesn't know her anymore. And if you are so sure that I don't know her, then why are you even here? Oh wait, I'll answer that. You're trying to trap her into coming back to you when all she wants is her freedom. But I'm sure you knew that. Since you know her so well."

"Freedom means she doesn't want you either ."

"Don't be so sure. I'm giving her the space that she needs. But don't expect me to bow out. Unlike you, I love and value her. I'll wait as long as I have to. I'm not going anywhere. I'm giving her the space she needs. That's it. But you can be sure, her designated drawers in my bedroom are full and still there waiting.

"I'm warning you. Leave my wife alone."

"Good day, Mr. Williams."

"Clown...." he said under his breath.

I just laughed as I walked away.

Jones

After staying at my mom's house for a few days, I had gone to see my dad. I had been staying the night in my dad's apartment at the retirement village. It was more like an upscale condominium complex. My mom wanted to make sure he still had the best. His memory had been going for awhile. He still had more good days than bad. Which was a blessing in and of itself.

Mom had tried to keep him home with some help when she needed to go run errands or just take a break. He was so fiercely independent he would run them off. One night a neighbor, a doctor, brought my dad home in the middle of the night.

Apparently, he had woke and didn't know where he was. Thinking he had to get home, he left and tried to break into their home. He broke a window thinking that he had misplaced his keys. The doctor recognized what was going on, thank God, and brought him home.

It scared my mom so much, the next day she was dragging us around town looking at places where dad can be properly cared for, but still have his independence. We found it here. I was up making my dad's favorite. French toast. It was as good as my mom's. She taught me how. I needed him to remember me always. I heard him coming out of his room. I knew he would recognize me. Even on bad days, he knew me.

"Jones. Is that French toast I smell?"

"Mom's recipe."

"Then it's the best."

"Just like her."

"I second that. Now, let's talk." He said, sitting at the table.

"About?"

"Not that I mind. I've actually enjoyed the company. But you being here the last couple of night's has brought on some questions."

"Always questions with you." I joked.

"You don't ask, you won't know."

"True. So, shoot..."

"Who's seeing to your accounts at work?"

"Jackson is. I'm taking a break with all of this Bobbi drama going on."

"You need it. That girl never did quite fall in line the way I thought she would, did she?"

"I guess not." I answered as I plated our food.

I changed the subject when I sat down. Making small talk. I just wanted to be near him.

"You seem different." He told me.

"Maybe I am dad."

"Nothing wrong with change."

I shrugged my shoulders. Inside I thought to myself, that depends. I took a deep breath and turned my chair to face him.

"Dad..."

"Yeah, Jones."

"I just want you to know and remember how much I love and admire you. Always."

"Uh oh. I know what this is. I'm dying, aren't I?"

"No dad. Nothing like that. You're going to be fine. You are strong. And mom has you. So, she'll be ok too."

I could tell his grip on reality was changing as I was speaking. That was ok. I had said what I needed to. I knew he would remember it. I did the dishes and then went into the bedroom to change for court. I put on a suit. Even though what I wore wouldn't matter much. I brushed my newly cut hair. Gargled and brushed my teeth.

I placed my feet in my new Florshiems, and then pulled another shoe box from under the bed. Opening it to reveal a silver handgun. Dad made sure we knew how to hunt and protect our homes. In the case we ever needed to. I made sure the rounds were in place. Put it on safety and tucked it in my monogrammed gun holster.

Before I left, I hugged my father for a long time. By now, he didn't recognize things. Only me. His patient care assistant was there by now. Turning to her before I left, I gave her instructions.

"Patti. No news for the next couple of days. Trumps' running the U.S. into the ground and it's upsetting dad. Turn it to the tennis channel. Let him watch Venus and Serena run all over the competition."

"Ok." she said with a smile.

"Oh. And tell him everyday how much I love him.."

She agreed but gave me a strange look. I didn't care. Nothing mattered anymore. Least of all how people looked at me. I had to get going. I had an appointment to keep. As I sat in my driver's seat, I told Siri to call my brother. He didn't answer, so I left him a message.

Hey Jack. It's your little brother. I'm headed to court today. Which you know. By the end of the day, everything will be different. I just wanted to tell you that I love you. You have always been my conscience. At times I've resented you for it. Though, you've never been wrong. You better save this message. You will never hear me say that again. Well, alright. I wish I could have spoken to you. In any case. I love you bro. I really do.

After disconnecting that call, I had her dial my sister. Her voice came on after one ring.

"Jones. Where have you been? I have been calling you."

"I was spending time with dad."

"Oh."

"Don't say it like that, Jazz."

"Like what?"

"Like I just said I was having Maker's Mark with Satan."

She giggled a little at that little joke.

"He's our dad, Jazz. With all of his imperfections, he has always loved us. Try to forgive him. And me as well."

"You know I will forgive you, Jones. You're my baby brother. I know your heart. I am not always ok with your choices, but I love you."

I took a deep breath. I needed to hear that someone in my life would always love and forgive me.

"Jones. What's wrong baby boy?"

"Nothing sis. I just needed to hear that. But hey. I'm almost at the courthouse so, I'm going to let you off here."

"Do you need me to come?" she offered

"No! No. What I do need you to do is get Jack and go to mom's house. She is going to need you two."

"Need us? For what?"

"She's just not taking this well. You know how she is. Protect the family name and all. I'm afraid I'm an embarrassment. With the divorce and everything."

"Oh, yeah. Alright. We'll swing by at lunchtime and wait for you to update us on how everything went. Is that good?"

"Yeah. It's good. Now listen, kiss all the kids and tell them Uncle Jonesy loves them. And you too."

"Alright. Be safe. Bye."

After we hung up, I almost changed my mind. Almost. Thinking of how this would affect my family did make me feel a little guilty. It was not going to be enough to change my plans though. I had left mom a letter in her makeup table to find, eventually. The fact of the matter is I couldn't change course now. Unlike some people, I took my vows seriously. Until death do us part.

Bobbi, Kelvin and Jones

I had spent the entire night pacing the floor. I felt bad for keeping Kelvin from sleeping. But I was nervous. I hadn't seen Jones since the day I had the restraining order extended. This was the goal, of course.

The issue was, I knew him. He needed to have control. Me leaving and not coming back was a huge loss of control for him. Kenna told me that he had approached her at court. He was obviously coming undone.

Kelvin insisted on going with me. Finally, at 0200, he gave me one of my Xanax. It helped to calm me and I eventually fell asleep. I awoke to him shaving and singing in the bathroom. He seemed happier than I was about the divorce. After lying there and enjoying my serenade and dreading the day to come as well, I rolled out of the bed and got ready to go.

I was quiet the whole morning. I just had a sinking feeling. If it were a scary movie, the music just before Freddy jumped out would be playing. Kelvin held my hand the whole ride there. He brought me so much peace and comfort.

We pulled up to the courthouse and found a spot across the street from the entrance. He came around and opened my door.

"Are you ready?" He asked.

"Well now, that remains to be seen."

He kissed my forehead and my hand and we started to walk towards the entrance. As we started up the walk, I saw him running up out the corner of my eye before he even spoke.

"Bobbi!!!!! You made me do this!!!" He yelled out as he brought the gun up.

I heard the loud bang of the gun going off. I closed my eyes and said a prayer. I fully expected to open them and find myself receiving a heavenly tour from St. Peter. To be totally transparent, for a split second, I was at peace. No more pain or living in fear. I had wanted that for so long, no matter how it came to me.

Instead, I felt myself almost being thrown across the lawn of the courthouse. Just as I opened my eyes, I saw Jones put the gun to his head and pull the trigger.

I heard my screams, but I thought they came from someone else. As I tried to stand up, I found I couldn't. That was when I realized that Kelvin was lying across me. I said his name, to no response. I then started to shake him and scream his name. I rolled him over and saw blood on his shirt. I tried to put pressure on where I saw the blood.

I couldn't tell if he was even breathing. My next though was to immediately get started doing CPR. I didn't even know if I should be, but I decided it couldn't hurt. By now, there was a crowd gathering. Police were running in and I heard sirens getting closer. The ambulance arrived and the paramedics had to pull me off of him. I was in shock. This was my fault. He was here with a bullet in him, fighting for his life because of me.

I saw another ambulance load Jones in. A medic was sitting on his chest pumping and counting as another was squeezing something over his face. I had a split second to decide who to ride with. I ran over to the ambulance holding Kelvin and was helped in by the medic.

They cut his shirt off of him and hooked him up to machines. They found the source of the bleeding. It was his right side. They applied pressure dressings to stop the bleeding. They started an IV and all I could do was watch and pray. This had to be a bad dream.

One of the medics turned to me and asked me about Kelvin. I told them he was a doctor with no allergies, no medical issues and no religious preferences that would affect his care. Just then the medic noticed I was bleeding as well. There was a scrape on my forehead, but I had also been grazed by the bullet on my arm. If Kelvin hadn't of pushed me as he jumped in front of the bullet, it would have hit me in my chest and I would surely be dead.

They separated us in the ER. I needed to be tended to as well and they had to work on him. I asked every nurse, tech and doctor what was going on with him. Eventually, a nurse took pity on me and I was told he was up in surgery and that they would keep me posted.

My arm injury was a little worse then initially thought. I would require stitches. Once they were done treating my arm like a ripped shirt button, they gave me something for pain and nerves. This was followed up by a shot to stop infection. Next, I was sent to X-ray. When I arrived back to my room, Tina, Kenna and a policeman were waiting for me.

"Thank God.." Tina said as she hugged me.

Kenna had tears in her eyes and hugged me as well. After what seemed like forever, they let go. Kenna then spoke.

"When we pulled up to the courthouse there were police everywhere. They were putting up yellow tape and wouldn't let us through. Then Tina saw your pocketbook on the grass. We immediately started calling hospitals."

"He shot Kelvin..." I managed to get out.

Just then the officer spoke.

"Ma'am we have some questions for you about what happened at the courthouse..."

Kenna interrupted, "ONLY, if you're up for it. I'm her attorney." She told him as she handed him her card.

"I'm fine. I can talk." And I told the officer everything that I could remember. It was then I remembered to ask about my husband. The man who had done this. The man who had tried to kill me only hours earlier.

"I'm sorry ma'am. He did not survive his injuries." The officer told me.

He then handed me Jones wallet and wedding band in a plastic bag. I thought I was going to be sick. I didn't know what to do. After everything he had done, I still didn't want him to die. Now he was gone, and I was finally safe, but I didn't feel that way. I just went numb. I stopped speaking and retreated into my own head.

"I think that's all for now, officer." Kenna said.

He agreed, left his card in case I thought of anything else and left. If I thought the surprises were over, I was sorely mistaken. The doctor caring for me came in.

"Bobbi, I know it's been a trying day. But, can you tell me how far along you are?"

I just stared at him, confused. Tina gasped and Kenna said, "Far along in what?"

"Your pregnancy. We give all women of childbearing age pregnancy test when they come in. Yours was positive in blood and urine."

We all looked at him as if he was speaking another language.

"Alrighty then. I can tell that you're all surprised. I'll grab the ultrasound machine and we'll find out together."

With that he left us there. All quiet and all in shock. Pregnant. I couldn't believe it. And Kelvin was upstairs in surgery. I prayed he made it through. There was no way he could leave me here to raise this baby by myself.

The doctor came back, and as sure as the day was long, there was a baby on that monitor. Heartbeat and all. I was almost twelve weeks. I hadn't felt sick or anything. I had just been, me. I broke down and cried. Tina and Kenna too. As the doctor was leaving, he turned to me once more.

"Dr. Lindsay is out of surgery and in recovery. The bullet missed his organs. His injuries are serious. However, there was no damage done that can't be healed in time."

"Thank God. Thank you doctor."

"When he wakes up, I'll have you taken to see him by wheelchair. I still want to observe you, especially now."

I nodded and he left. Now, how was I going to tell Kelvin that he was going to be a dad?

Tina and Cade

It took me a moment to recognize where I was when I opened my eyes. I looked around and thought, "Crap." I was at our house, in our bed with Cade's head on my stomach and his arms wrapped around my waist. The way we had slept after making love since college.

I lifted my head and it fell back against the pillow, heavily. I definitely had a hangover. Last night's events started coming back to me. I had such a great time in England. I thought I had made up my mind. After thinking about it and talking to my older sister, I had decided to actually try to give our marriage a shot.

She and her husband had been married for just shy of twenty years. They were high school sweethearts who were married at seventeen and nineteen. They had survived all sorts of trials, infidelity being one. She said now she was happy she had stuck it out. She encouraged me to do the same.

So, as a start, I accepted his tickets to Spring Jam. I mean what girl doesn't want to see Sammy, Wale, Miguel, Carl Thomas, Elle Varner, Teedra Moses and Tank. He had even made sure that we had backstage access and hung out with them after the show.

We had drinks, and even went to a private after party. We poured ourselves into the car at around 0400 and as our driver took us home, we started getting cozy. Cade kissed me over and over, whispering how much he loved, missed and needed me. His hands started to travel up my dress and I didn't stop him.

We headed straight to the bedroom and had, though I hated to admit it, the best sex we had ever had. Now, in the light of day, I wasn't sure how to feel. I mean, it was good, and he was my husband. Why then did I feel a twang of guilt? I knew why. Because I couldn't stop thinking about Larry. I was stuck and confused.

As I lie there, Cade woke up and lifted his head to look at me.

"Good morning Tutu." He said with a little hoarseness in his voice. That was my nickname he gave me in college as well. The first time he saw me dance ballet I had on a purple tutu. He never let it go.

"Ugghhh....not so loud...good morning." I returned.

He laughed at me as he leaned up, kissed me and then headed to the bathroom. He came back out with two Tylenol and a cup of water and handed them to me.

"You should stick to Pinot. You never could handle the harder stuff."

I took them, drank the water down to half and then handed the rest to him. He sounded like he needed it.

"Boy, why'd you let me drink so much?"

"It wasn't my fault. You and Elle made a bet over who could take the most Tequila shots."

"Oh, my goodness, Tequila. I'm gonna die." I said as I pulled the covers over my head.

He laughed and climbed in bed next to me. He hit the intercom button that connected us to the housekeeper's apartments.

"Beth.."

"Yes, Cade, I'm here."

"Tee needs hangover food."

"Chocolate chip pancakes and garbage omelettes. I have to run to the grocery store, but it'll be coming right up."

I groaned at just the sound of it, but it always worked. It was an omelette with beef and turkey scrapple, turkey sausage and bacon with homefries and cheese. I only ever ate like that on the rare occasion I was hungover.

"Thank you, Beth." he said before letting the button go and turning his focus back to me.

He started to kiss my neck and back. He rubbed my body with his unusually soft hands, for a ball player anyway. I forgot how his body rubs had always relaxed me.

"I missed you so much." He whispered. He then moved closer to me. Pressing himself against me.

"Hello" I said...

"See what you do to me?"

"About last night..."

"Yeah, about it. It was great."

"It may have been premature. We're just starting to work on us." I said as I rolled over into his broad chest. I don't know if we should complicate things by having sex."

He wrapped his arms around me and moved in so close, that we were sharing the same air.

"See, it's not complicated to me. You're my wife. I love you. I messed up and I take responsibility for it. But I need you back...in every way."

"Cade..."

"Every. Way. I promise you. I haven't been with anyone since I left for camp. I need you to believe that."

I looked at his face and into his eyes. I always knew when he was lying. And dang it if he wasn't telling me the truth. I didn't know if it made me feel better or worse. I took a deep breath.

"I do believe you. But, there's something I should tell you."

He pressed his mouth on mine before I could say another word and kissed me. I thought I should resist, but I didn't. There was something, familiar and comforting in his kiss. After a few minutes of that, he took my face in his hands.

"Please don't say it. I already know. But I don't think I can hear you say the words. As long as you aren't in love with him, it's fine. I saw the way you looked at each other at mediation. My heart almost fell out my chest. For once, I knew how you felt, and it was the worse feeling in the world. I don't know how you survived it so many times..."

"It hurts less each time. When it doesn't hurt anymore. You know it's over."

"I hate to ask because the last thing I ever want to do is hurt you."

"Yes and no. " I knew what he wanted to know, so I started to speak so he didn't have to ask it. "It definitely didn't hurt as much as the first time. But it stung..."

"Stung.?"

"Yes."

"Well. I guess that's something." he said, kissing my hand.

"I guess. But I don't know what. And I don't want to lead you on. If we keep doing this, we may both end up hurt.."

He thought for a moment.

"I understand. And thank you for being honest. But, I'm a big boy." he said as he pressed against me again, making me laugh. "I've made my bed and if you decide you don't want to stay, I'll lie in it. As I promised. But right now, in our bed, in our home, with no more lies between us, I need my wife and best friend."

This time when he kissed me, I let him. He didn't stop kissing me. Wherever there was skin you could find his hands and mouth. He turned me on my stomach and pulled me onto my knees. He then turned on his back and laid with his face between my legs. I grabbed the cushioned headboard so tightly as he licked and sucked that my hand prints were left there.

I moved back and forth on his tongue as he held me strongly by my waist. He treated me as if I were his last supper. This went on for so long I lost track of how many orgasms he caused me to have. Someone must have been practicing. I didn't want to think about it. I had to be honest though. It was way better than I remembered.

He then climbed onto his knees, pushed my back down so that my stomach was flat against the bed, and entered me. He yelled out and dug his nails into my back. With each stroke we both came closer and closer to climax. When he was seconds away he grabbed my neck and whispered that I was his, in my ear. I didn't argue. For now, at least, I was.

A few seconds later we both collapsed onto the bed. We lie there for a few moments. No words spoken. This possibly breaking up possibly working it out sex was awesome. I couldn't deny that. I started to doze off again with him lying on me the same way he had been when I woke. It was then we heard a knock on the door. We both laughed. We had forgotten about the hangover food. He covered both of us with the comforter and told Beth to come in.

She did with a huge smile on her face. She sat the breakfast tray across my lap and turned to leave. She then winked at me on the way out. I started to laugh, and he joined in. It felt nice to laugh with him again. Like we did in college. But there was still a feeling that nagged at me. I pushed it to the side. I would have to deal with it later. Right now, I needed hangover food.

Bobbi/Tina/Kenna

We were out at the store picking up some food and other supplies that I would need with Kelvin coming to stay with me after he was released. It was a quiet trip. I think we all had some things on our minds. I was tired of the silence. There was a coffee shop across the street from the store owned by a girl we went to school with, Tinsley. That was gonna have to do.

"I don't know what's going on, but we're headed to Tinsley's to talk." I said as we packed the car. I was glad I had already bought ice cream, so we had time for a chat before I needed to get the food home.

We got a booth in the back. I ordered Orange passionfruit tea. Kenna ordered white hot chocolate and Tina had caramel vanilla coffee. We all just sat there for awhile, quietly. That was out of the ordinary.

"Ok girls. What's up? We're all on mute. Someone talk, please. We are each other's sounding boards. Tee? How is it with you and Cade?" I asked to break the ice.

She sat back in her chair and took a deep breath. "We slept together..."

I almost choked on my tea and Kenna almost dropped her hot chocolate.

"You what and huh?" Kenna asked.

"I know...and it was spectacular....it was after the Spring Jam. He just said all the things I think I wanted to hear from him at the moment."

"What about Larry?" I asked.

"I have no clue. I have been mulling it over, believe me. I actually feel guilty. As if I'm cheating on Larry with Cade."

"I'm confused. I thought you said you wanted freedom to be with Larry in England." I put out there.

"Right. Then I talked to Claudia..."

Kenna and I both sighed at that. We loved her big sister, but she was not someone who gave the best advice.

"I know. But she told me I would regret it if I didn't try everything to save my marriage. I started to doubt myself." She confessed.

Kenna leaned up, took Tina's hand and spoke.

"Listen. You know whatever you do we will support you. Let me remind you that you have done everything you could to try and save your marriage. You forgave him, prayed, went to counseling and anything else that a wife would do to save her marriage. Sometimes it works out and sometimes it doesn't. Now, if Cade makes you happy and you want to try again you know we have your back. But do it because it's what you want to do and it's what's best for you."

"Thanks girl. He left to go back on the road. He only had a few weeks off. The season started and he's traveling with the team. It'll give me time to think. Without great sex from him OR Larry to trip me up. I need to choose."

"Don't forget, it's okay to choose yourself too babe." I added.

She took a deep breath, nodded and sipped her coffee.

"You're both right. I'm so blessed to have my girls. And, nobody called me a slut..."

"Night is still young...." Kenna added.

We all laughed at that. She knew she was nowhere near that. He was her husband and she hadn't slept with Larry since before mediation.

"Enough of my soap opera, what's up with you, Bobbi? Is little baby Tina making you sick?" she asked me.

"Tina??...Tuh...I think one of you is enough." We all laughed again. I then started talking.

"I think I've just been mourning Jones. It's weird, right? After everything he put me through. I mean he tried to kill me after all..." The tears started after I said that. Kenna reached over to hug me. Tina held my hand. It gave me the strength to keep talking.

"I've been having nightmares. Even when I'm woke, like flashbacks. He's calling out that it's my fault and then he shoots himself." I started outright bawling.

Some people looked over as they comforted me. Kenna gave those watching me the "mind ya business look", and they turned back around.

She then came to kneel down in front of me.

"Listen. Jones was a huge part of your life. Good and bad. Mostly bad, but part of it all the same. Of course, you're in mourning. You're also having some PTSD it seems like to me. So, we'll get you into counseling. You're one of the strongest people I know."

"A survivor..." Tina added through her own tears.

"She's not wrong. Now. If you need to go see Jones, to ease your mind and be sure he's gone, you know we're with you...whatever you need, we got you. So does Kelvin. But most importantly, we need you AND baby safe. Ok?" she told me

I nodded my head...and wiped my face.

"You're right." I told them.

"Duh..." Tina said as she rubbed my belly. Which was no longer flat.

"Is Doc happy about the baby?" She asked.

"He doesn't know yet."

"What??" Kenna said.

"What do you mean??" Tina added.

"He's got a lot to deal with. And what if he doesn't want me. I mean, I'm the reason he's hurt..."

"Absolutely not..." Kenna assured me.

"Don't even think it. You are not...I repeat NOT responsible for this. And I'm sure Kelvin feels the same way. That man loves you and he is going to love our baby." Tina added.

I nodded and wiped my tears again. Kenna kept staring at me...I finally asked her what she was looking at.

"Your makeup. You've been bawling for thirty minutes and not a smear. Is that RiRi's? I'm going home to cry in mine to test it out..."

We all burst out laughing. We stayed about fifteen more minutes, then headed out. Back to our usual selves and singing "Sorry, not Sorry" on the way to my house to finish fixing it up for Kelvin to come home.

Kelvin and Bobbi

It had been over two weeks since the shooting. She had left the funeral planning to Jones's family. He had tried to kill her after all. She was often times quiet. I knew she was replaying everything in her head. She was scheduled to start therapy in the next couple of weeks. She had been through so much. It was time for her to find some peace, with me. I would be there the whole way.

I sat on the couch watching TV at Bobbi's condo. She wouldn't hear of me being released to my bachelor's pad when I needed so much care. The bullet hadn't hit any organs, Thank God. But I still needed to heal. This included dressing changes, drains, pain meds and antibiotics.

Bobbi had even learned how to tend to my drains and change my dressings before we left the hospital. I still had a nurse come and check on me three times a week. She said that Bobbi was doing such a good job she should split her pay with her. My parents were in another state. She kept them informed the whole way. They would be coming out soon to see me.

It was my birthday and I didn't much feel like celebrating. Bobbi cooked. She made Shrimp, scallops and red snapper. Mashed potatoes with cheese and asparagus. The girl could cook too. I was wondering what it was she couldn't do. She helped me into the dining room and sat my plate in front of me. We said grace and then started to eat. At least I did. She was just pushing her food around on the plate and sipping tea.

"Aren't you hungry babe?"

"Oh, I nibbled the whole time I was cooking. I'm just making some room."

"Ok..."

I noticed that in the corner was her easel with a portrait covered by a sheet.

"What's that?" I asked.

"Oh, it's part of your birthday gift."

"I told you not to get me anything. I just wanted to be with you today. That's enough."

"I know. Technically, I painted it, so I didn't get you anything." She explained using her own brand of logic.

"You love finding loopholes." I said as we laughed together.

"Well, can I see it?"

"Sure, go unveil it." She said. I looked at her and she seemed nervous. She probably thought I wouldn't like it. Sensitive artist, I thought.

I stood and walked slowly over to it. I took the cover off and then stood back a couple of feet to take it all in. It was a portrait of the two of us. That was plain. We were surrounded by baby toys, diapers, and everything you can imagine a baby needing. I then focused on her. In the portrait her belly was more of a ball with writing on it.

I read and re-read it. "It's a boy." It finally hit me what she was trying to tell me. I turned around so quick I thought I tore some stitches. She was standing behind me with a little square box.

"No way.."

"Here. Open it..." she told me. Nodding towards the box.

I opened the box and in it was an ultrasound dated a few days prior. Sure enough, it was a baby, our baby, and it was a boy. She lifted her shirt and there was no mistaking it. I looked at her in awe. I then reached out and touched her little belly. Slowly, as if I was afraid it would disappear. There weren't even words.

"Kelvin. Say something. Are you upset with me?"

"Upset? What are you talking about? I've never been happier. I'm going to be a dad. Come here."

I hugged her so hard I hurt myself. But I didn't care. I was going to be a dad.

"It says you're over three months. Almost four, actually. How long have you known?"

"I found out in the ER while you were in surgery."

"Yeah. Every woman gets a pregnancy test...." I said. The OB/GYN in me kicking in.

"Right. But I wanted to make sure you were getting better before I told you. Are you sure you're happy."

"I've never been this happy. I've always wanted a son. Look at you. More beautiful than ever. I didn't think that possible. Little Kelvin Junior."

"Or Bobby J." she added.

"Maybe next time." I teased her.

"Oh, you're already talking about more babies."

"Of course. We can't stop at one. I've always wanted my children close in age so they could be buds. Play and plot against us together." I told her, smiling at just the thought of it.

"I'm still stuck on this more babies thing..."

She said as we held each other and laughed. I just couldn't stop thinking that I would give her everything, just like she was giving me.

Tina and Cade

I was counting down the days until Cade came back. We needed to talk, in person. My girls were right. I needed to make a choice. I had been thinking about me lately and less about Cade and Larry. Who was I? I had been Cade's wife and before that, his girl. I spent all of the years you spend getting to know yourself, supporting him.

I was so different than the person I was from eighteen to thirty-one. In some respects, I knew me, in others, I had no clue. For example, I had stopped dancing to travel with him. I could have been the next Misty. Who knew. I had offers from three ballet companies when he was drafted.

There were other things as well. I decided that the time I needed was not to fix my marriage, but to get to know me. Now I had to tell Cade. I waited in the home which held a mix of memories for me. I remembered him surprising me with it. It was twenty thousand square feet. It held eight bedrooms and ten bathrooms. There were two kitchens, a wine cellar, an indoor AND outdoor pool with a two bedroom, two bathroom poolhouse, where Beth stayed. I had loved it so much. It had everything I ever wanted. It was the culmination of all our dreams, sacrifices and hard-work. I couldn't wait to start filling it with babies.

Not long after, the trouble began. Pictures of him in the blogs kissing women started. He had an excuse for it all. It was embarrassing. Everyone knew he was married. I was with him for red carpet events. Smiling like an idiot and pretending everything was ok. Then came the bold mistresses, calling and emailing me. Each one hurt a little less, just as I told him. Now I was numb to it and more than ready to move on. It was time to stop this mess, for good.

He came in and called out. "Tutu, it smells good in here girl. Where you at?"

"In the kitchen..."

He strolled in and started looking in pots and stealing food.

"Boy, stop. It's almost done. Go wash your hands."

"Okay, okay.."

He went to the bathroom to do like I said as I made plates and sat them on the table. I then opened his favorite wine, Carbonere, from the Va. Beach winery and poured him a glass. I had the Son of a Peach. He came back in, kissed my neck and sat across from me.

"No Tequila?" He joked.

"Haha.." I said with a smile.

"Fried chicken, salmon, brussel sprout mac and cheese, salad, all my favorites. If you tell me you're pregnant it'll be the icing on the cake." He said, only half joking.

"Obviously, you've already been drinking." I joked with him.

He dug in and we made small talk. When he was done eating, I started in.

"I remember when you bought me this home. I thought I was so blessed. And I was. It was everything. You were everything to me. I never thought you would ever break me."

"Tina." he said as he reached to hold my hand. I let him. I think I needed him to.

"But you did break me. And you broke us. I tried so hard to save us. You didn't want it. You thought I would always be here, waiting. For awhile, you were right. I was a fool, your fool..." I stopped to take a breath. This was so hard. Because I did still love him.

"Tee, I know I messed up. Just give me a chance to fix it. To fix us."

"See, that's the problem. You had chances. So many chances. You chose not to take advantage of them. Now, I'm done. And I don't want you to waste anymore time or effort. It won't change anything."

"You promised to try, Tee. For three months, it's barely been two..."

"I guess, for the first time, I'm breaking my promise to you. Believe me, I know how that feels. You can tie me up in court, I don't care, I just want to be happy. And I can't be that with you any longer. I don't even know if I can be it with me."

"What does that mean?"

"I can't remember a time that I wasn't yours. Now, I need to be mine. Learn who I am without you. So, I'm going to do something I've wanted to do since I was a little girl."

"Travel..." he said quietly.

"Yes, you remembered."

"Yes, I remember. I remember everything about you. I'm in love with you. Always have been. I probably always will be."

"Cade. I won't sit here and pretend that I don't love you anymore. I do. I almost wish I didn't. It would make this a lot easier. It's breaking my heart as it is. But I have to choose me. For the first time."

He sat there staring. He looked small to me, which wasn't easy for him. I stood, kissed his cheek, grabbed my purse and my shoes, and left him there. In that grand house that had become my prison of broken promises. And for the first time, I felt totally free.

Tina and Larry

I drove over to Larry's office a few days later. I had already made an appointment. I made sure to be the last of the day. I walked in and saw him sitting there. I locked the door behind me. He looked surprised to see me.

"Tina, I have an appointment in a few..."

"With Ms. Loveless....nice to meet you." I said with a smirk.

"That was you?"

"Yes. I needed to see you..."

"What about Cade and the agreement?"

"Well, I hope you're ready to be tied up in court, counselor. Because I don't want to spend another day like this."

"Tina...like what?" he asked.

"A stranger..to myself."

"You are being super cryptic.." Poor baby looked confused. Join the club.

"Right???...ok. You know I've only ever known Cade, until you."

"I am aware."

He looked at me so intensely, I could barely stand it.

"Goodness, I've missed you."

"I've missed you too, Tina. You have no idea."

That made telling him a little harder.

"Ok. I wanted to tell you, in person, that I'm leaving."

"Leaving? What are you talking about?"

"I've lost me. I need to take some time by myself. So, I'm going to travel for the next month or so."

He shook his head. "With Cade?"

"No. Alone. There is no more Cade and Tina. That's all I've ever been. I need to learn who I am, alone. Do you understand what I'm saying?"

"Yes. I actually do get it. I think you're right. It's a good idea."

He surprised me by how calm he was. He came over and sat in front of me on the corner of his desk.

"Oh ok. well, I thought that before I leave, I should be honest with you. You are all I've been thinking about. You have taught me so much. You have treated me like a woman is supposed to be treated and I...."

"You what?"

"I don't know if this trip will get me back to where I need to be. But it's a step. And, I love you..."

He sat there stoically for a moment. Then a smile started to spread across his face. Starting from his eyes.

"Bout time, woman..."

"For what?" Now I was the one looking lost.

"That you told me how you feel. Waiting for you was almost the end of me. Now I have renewed motivation..."

"Motivation to do what?"

"To wait for you."

"You want to wait for me to finish traipsing across the globe. Trying to find myself and learning to be whole?" I asked.

"Listen. I know myself and I'd like to think I know you. I understand why you need this, and I support it. You say you aren't whole. Well, I'll take half of you over someone I'm just tolerating all of anyday. I want you, and I'm waiting..."

I couldn't do anything but smile. Someone thought I was worth waiting for. It sent chills through me.

"So where are you headed?" He asked as he sat next to me.

"I thought I'd start in Ghana. The city of Kumasi is said to be a hub of culture..."

Jeffrey and Kenna

"Ok, that was crazy." Jeff said as we left out the theatre from seeing Acrimony.

"Really? I looked at it as more of a cautionary tale."

"Yes, darling you would, wouldn't you? You being a woman and all."

We both laughed on our way to his car.

"Are you hungry?" He asked.

"I could eat."

"As can I. Where to, my lady?"

"Oh, there's this Japanese steakhouse that I love."

Just as I was speaking he pulled me close and kissed me. The first thing I thought was *"Damn."* His lips were soft and he smelled like peppermint and...*man. I loved it.* I then remembered that we worked together. I started to pull away, but I didn't. I wrapped my arms around him and kissed him back. We finally tore ourselves away when a group of college kids started clapping and yelling for us.

"What was that counselor?" I asked as I made no effort to escape his embrace.

"My ticket out of the friend zone. I want you to be clear on my intentions. I love spending time with you. And I will never be that mate that you tell to turn around while you pick out clothes to take another chap on a date.." he explained.

"What?!? I said as I laughed.

"Never mind, are we clear?" He inquired in a serious voice.

"Crystal.."

"Good. Now, where is this Steakhouse?"

"Not too far."

We arrived and were fortunate enough to be seated at a grill with just the two of us instead of the eight to ten people who usually sit at each table. It was getting pretty close to closing time so the chef cooked for just us to.

He made hearts with the rice and even poured our wine for us. I was enjoying myself and Jeffrey seemed to be as well. As soon as the chef completed our show and served up our food, he left us alone. I watched Jeffrey for a moment. He was so, refined. There was an air about him that went beyond being professional. I then realized, we talked a lot about work, but everything else was surface. I had questions. So, I started the conversation.

"Tell me about yourself." I said out of nowhere.

"You know me."

"I know Jeff, the funny lawyer and friend. You kissed me tonight, in a very non-friend zone type of way, to quote you."

"I did. Did it work? Is that why you're asking, love."

"It definitely didn't not work." I said with a coy smile.

"Then Larry was right. Good on him, for me of course."

"Larry? Oh. Now you and Larry are talking about me behind my back?" I asked with feigned irritation. What about?"

"Right, we talked about what I'd need to do to take this friendship further. Contrary to popular belief, we men do not relish being in the friend zone."

"And he told you to kiss me as a way out?" I asked as I took another sip of Pinot.

"Not in those exact words, no. The kiss was all me. I'd wanted to do that for quite awhile really."

"Well...What did he say?"

"I told the bloke how I felt about you. Not that it wasn't obvious to everyone..."

"It wasn't obvious to me."

"Because all you see are briefs and settlement offers."

"Is that a bad thing?" I wanted to know.

"You love what you do. Nothing bad about that now is it? Except, I know you want more."

"More?"

"Yes. Love, children, the house on the proverbial hill, the whole bloody dream."

"No, you're right. I do want it all." I admitted.

"Don't we all, darling. Well, I want all of you, in any case."

"All of me. Well, how much you get of me depends on how well you let me get to know you."

"I'm up for it. What would you like to know then?"

"Where did you grow up?"

I could tell in his eyes that he was thinking. He drank a bit of his wine before he answered.

"England." He answered shortly.

"Smartass..."

We both laughed.

"Alright, outside of Lincolnshire, mostly."

"Country or city?"

"Bit of both if I'm honest. But mainly country." He said, taking another sip and looking a little uncomfortable.

"Did you like it there?"

"When I was able to have my freedom, yes. It was lovely."

When he said it, there was look in his eyes. I couldn't place it. I didn't know if good or bad memories were being stirred.

"Your freedom?"

"Strict parents and all that..."

"Oh. Yeah, mine were too.

"What about school? And if you say Oxford..." I warned his smartass.

He laughed and moved a little closer to me, which I found I wanted more than I even knew.

"Marlborough college, you would know it as a boarding school."

"Boarding school? And why does that one sound so familiar?"

"Right, Have you heard of Kate Middleton?"

"I have eyes and ears, so yes."

"Right, her alma mater as well, as it were."

"Wow. So you're like, posh..."

He laughed out loud at that.

"Good grief I hope not. Mum and dad had friends who knew friends. I was able to get in."

"Oh. Connections. Got it..."

We stayed there talking until we looked around and realized there were only ten minutes until closing. They were mopping the floor in the table seating sections. I hadn't noticed anything but his eyes and smile for the last hour. He had definitely made it out of the friend zone.

Cade and Larry

My secretary came into my office with a worried look on her face.

"What's wrong? Did you schedule a meeting and forget to put it on my calendar again?" I teased her.

"No, and that only happened once...twice...." she answered, correcting herself.

"Well why do you look like you have a secret? What's up?" I wanted to know. She was looking very suspicious and I wasn't a fan of intrigue.

"Well, Mr. Williams is here. The ball player. I know him because I'm a die-hard basketball fan." She admitted.

"Lakers?" I threw out there.

"Heck no. My father would disown me. Sixers..." she informed with a smile.

"I should have asked you that before I hired you." I teased.

"Ha Ha. Anyway, he's not on the schedule. Should I send him in?"

"Uhh. That depends. Do I have anything pending?" I needed to know.

"No..."

"Then sure, but get his autograph first.." I told her with a smile, which she returned, mouthing her thanks on the way out.

He came walking in and immediately started checking out my office. He didn't even speak. He walked over to my wall with my degrees and newspaper articles of big- name cases that I've won. He carefully inspected each one. I kept reading and making notes on the brief I was examining.

His next stop was over to my bookcase. I knew what had drawn his eye. Tina had sent me postcards from Ghana, South Africa and Scotland. He picked up the one from Scotland.

"She always wanted to see castles. Live in one actually. I guess she's made it happen. The seeing them part." He said with a sad ass look on his face.

"I guess so." I agreed with him.

He put it down and finally sat in the chair on the other side of my desk. Now that he was ready to talk, I put down my pen and closed the brief.

"Mr. Williams, I have to advise you, again, against speaking without your attorney present." I started off.

"Noted."

"Ok. Now, I know you didn't come to offer me decorating advice. Now, what can I help you with?" I inquired, leaning back in my chair.

"Did you know it's unethical for a lawyer to develop a relationship with a client?" he wanted to know.

So that's what he wanted. Ok. I could play along.

"Sure. IF it affects the counsel given to the client."

"What you mean is, if you let's just for instance say, encouraged my wife to go through with the divorce so that you two could be together. Would that count?" he countered.

"Absolutely. If we had ever had that conversation. Which we never did."

He stared at me looking for some hint of fear. There was none. When he saw he failed to intimidate me, he started speaking again.

"Well, that's not what I came here for." He began. Dropping his threatening posture he had been using to try and rattle me.

"Do you mind sharing why you are here? I'm pretty busy." I told him, leaning back up and picking up a pen to begin writing again.

"I came here to tell you to treat her right. Make her happy and give her everything she needs."

"That's the plan."

Now this did surprise me.

"She's a good girl. I took that forgranted. Don't do the same thing." He cautioned me.

"I won't."

"Because you never know who will be in the wings waiting to do what you won't."

"Well, since there's nothing I wouldn't do for her, I don't have to worry about that."

He just nodded his head at that. He stared at me and I met his eyes. He then stood up.

"I believe that..."

"It's the truth..."

"I also believe she's going to break your heart. She will never get over me. And you showed up too quick. I know her. She needs time." He warned me.

"Correction. You knew her."

"Right. I knew her. It also looks like she's running around trying to find something. If she could find it in you, she would either be here, or you would be over there with her."

What he said did send a little pang through me. That's because what he said had crossed my mind as well. I wasn't about to let him know that. He was trying to rattle me. It also wasn't any of his business."

"Was there a reason you were here? Maybe I missed it in all of your talking about things that don't concern you." I let him know.

"I can see I cut you deep. Fine. You'll be hearing from my lawyer soon. I'm giving her everything she wants. She's earned it." He told me.

"I'll be waiting."

"That's funny. So will I." he threw back at me.

With that, he turned and walked out. I sat back in my chair and thought for a moment. I then stood up, walked over to my shelf and picked up the same postcard. She had them made from pictures she took during her travels. This one was a picture of Stirling castle in Scotland. There was Elmina Castle from Ghana on the postcard next to it and the Egyptian museum on the other.

She had written on them as well. She thought it would be romantic to do this. And it was. I turned the one from Scotland over and read it for what seemed to be the hundredth time.

"It's just as beautiful here as I thought it would be. I've been having the best time and learning so much. But everytime I see something that takes my breath away, I think of you. Something I love, a sunset, sunrise, black sand, same. I miss you with my whole being. I'll be back soon...
Love Tina"

It must have torn him up to read this. But he still wants her to be happy. He's gained my respect. For that, at least. I sat the postcard down and went back to work. Mentally marking down the days until she was back, with me.

Bobbi/Tina/Kenna

"Noo...not there." I stopped Kenna from putting glasses in the wrong cabinet.

"But there are already glasses in there. Why not these?" she wanted to know.

"Those are decorative glasses. They go on the open shelves."

"Oh my goodness girl.." she whined.

"I told her worrisome tail to hire Laney back as her decorator. But noooo. She came back from finding herself and wants to find her own style too..." Bobbi said from the couch.

We gave her the job of opening the boxes and putting light knick knacks away. She said we were babying her because she was pregnant. She was right. After we finished the kitchen, we sat on my back patio to get some air. I loved the condo, but I was ready to move back into a home. This one was way smaller than what I was used to. It was only me after all. I loved it. Four bedroom, four baths, a pool and near town but not too far from the beach.

"Hey I have an idea." Bobbi said as we settled in.

"What's up?" Kenna asked.

"I want to open a shelter for domestic abuse survivors."

We both looked at her for a second to be sure we had heard her correctly.

"What? Bad idea?" She asked.

"Not at all..." I said.

"Are you sure you're ready to take that on?" Kenna asked.

"If I wait until I'm ready, I'd never do it. And someone out there can't afford to wait on me."

"I think it's a great idea. I had an idea myself. I wanted to open a dance studio. Maybe we can do scholarships for the kids of the survivors. Give them an outlet for their feelings. Who knows what they've seen?"

"Yessss...that would be so good for them." Bobbi added.

"Look at you two. I love it. I'll take care of the legal part, of course. Sidebar. I'm so glad you're getting back to dancing Tee."

"Right. You were so good."

"Thank you. I missed it. I was still actually taking classes when I could up until a couple of years ago. Getting back into shape is gonna kick my butt."

"You got this, girl. We are so proud of you. Finding what makes you happy, and we are here for it." Bobbi said with Kenna agreeing.

"I know y'all are. We sisters. That's how I know y'all gonna be here with me unpacking and decorating all weekend."

We all laughed.

"Now, Bobbi. Where were you thinking for the shelter?"

The gangs all here

We were all meeting at Kenna's favorite restaurant for her birthday. We had not all been together at once in about a month. We had started making a habit of all hanging out together as couples. We all got along great. We genuinely enjoyed each other's company. There had been a lot of changes in the last few months.

Bobbi was now seven months pregnant and sporting a huge wedding ring. She and Kelvin had eloped, with us as witnesses of course, and married on a beach in Jamaica a month earlier. Kelvin was determined his child be born to married parents. And he just adored Bobbi. We loved him for loving her. He was truly her hero. Though he liked to say that she saved him.

Larry and I were getting along great. Cade had changed his mind and decided to give me my divorce when I was traveling. I got the 13.5 million I was entitled to and we sold the house and split the profits. I was so happy to be free to be who I was or at least figure it out *and* with who I loved and most importantly who loved me. And that was Larry. We talked of our future often. But, even though I loved him, I wanted to take my time before jumping into another marriage. He was more than supportive. It just made me love him even more.

Today we sat around the grill, watching the chef make fire in onions and flip eggs on his utensils. The food was great. Dinner and a show. I could see why she loved this place. We ate and teased Bobbi because she couldn't drink. When we were just about done, Jeff stood up and clapped his hands asking for the attention of the whole restaurant. He then started to speak.

"Today is this beautiful young lady's birthday."

Customers all over started yelling out happy birthday to her. He let it go on for a few seconds. He then used his hands to quiet them down.

"Thank you, Thank you. Let me tell you about her. Besides the fact that she is obviously beautiful. She is patient, intelligent, kind, understanding and funny. She's also a bit of a cheeky little minx, which may well be the best part of her, if I'm honest..." he joked.

Bringing on more laughter and cheers at that.

She is everything a man could ask for. And she's all mine. So, none of you lot get any ideas."

Everyone there began to clap and then it died down. That's when he got down on one knee and produced an engagement ring. She was genuinely shocked. Her hands flew to her face and we were all cheering. He continued to speak.

"I remember telling you that one day, a man would see you for all you were, and make all your dreams come true. Right down to maternity leave. Well even back then, I spoke of myself. I have loved you for a long time. And now that I know your love, there's nothing else for me, is there. McKenna, my love. Will you do me the honor of being my wife?"

Through tears she yelled "Yess!!!" And threw her arms around him, almost knocking him backwards. She then turned to us showing her ring. We were all crying tears of happiness for her. This last year had been a journey for all of us. We learned ourselves and what we would and would not accept. And along the way, we learned what a man would and wouldn't do, if he loved you.

Don't Forget To Leave a Review Thank You Kindly

■■■

Follow Each of these friends on their own journey starting with Kenna.

Coming Soon

If He Loved You 2-Lies and Ladies

****

Other titles by this author

When He's Bad For You 1-3

When She's Bad For You 1(2-3 soon to come)

****

Contact this author:

DreamWakeWorkpublishing@Gmail.com

Fb: Author Asetah Dula

Instagram: AuthorTahDula

Twitter: @PsychT16

"

Made in the USA
Middletown, DE
20 July 2019